Lasting Legacy

JENIFER JENNINGS

Copyright © 2019 Jenifer Jennings

All rights reserved. Except as permitted under the U.S. Copyright Act of 1976, no part of this book may be reproduced or transmitted in any form or by any means, electronic or mechanical, including photocopying and recording, or by an information storage and retrieval system, without permission in writing from the publisher.

Editor: Jill Monday

Scripture quotations and paraphrases are taken from the Holy Bible, King James Version, Copyright © 1977, 1984, 2001 by Thomas Nelson, Inc.

This book is a work of historical fiction based closely on real people and events recorded in the Holy Bible. Details that cannot be historically verified are purely products of the author's imagination. Any resemblance to actual persons, living or dead, or actual events is purely coincidental.

For Allison and Patrick.

Chapter One

"And [Paul] came to Ephesus, and left them there: but he himself entered into the synagogue, and reasoned with the Jews." -Acts 18:19

A.D. 53, Ephesus

Lea stood at the end of Arcadian Street watching the waves lap against the stone wall of the bay. The salty sea breeze flung her dark hair around her face. Ships dotted the small canal of the Cayster River bringing their goods from across the Aegean Sea into the city and trading seafarers.

One ship caught her attention. As its crew unloaded, three passengers disembarked. A man who stood shorter than the other two was completely bald by a recent shoring. His clothes and style of beard indicated that he was a Jew. His presence almost shouted it like the lamps that lit up the columns of Arcadian Street at night. His companions were more humble in dress and presence. Though the woman that was among them had the pleated hair popular of a Roman citizen.

She glanced in Lea's direction and paused. Lea didn't recognize her, but the woman held her gaze as though trying to decipher her innermost thoughts.

The other man took the woman's hand and led her away from the ship. His gentle touch and guidance revealed their loving relationship.

Marriage. The thought reminded Lea of why she had ventured away from home that morning. She had come to the Agora to gather supplies and select a gift for her sister's wedding.

She gathered the loose folds of her dress and hurried up the crowded street. The gift she had chosen earlier that morning was safely tucked away in her bag, but she still needed to acquire the things her mother had requested. She took a right down Marble Road into the marketplace.

Makeshift booths filled the open space to capacity. Lea would have loved to browse every setup, but she had already used up her entire morning. She hurried through her shopping and paused only long enough at the sundial to see how much time her people-watching by the bay had cost her. If she stayed much longer, her mother might send her father out looking for her. Again.

She squeezed through the arches of the Gate of Mazeus and Mithridates. Their white marble glinted in the sunlight, but as soon as she passed under them the other side was made entirely of black marble.

Curetes Street led her home. The house bustled with activity in preparation for the wedding. The one-year anniversary of her sister's betrothal had come and gone and the family was waiting for the bridegroom to show himself any day.

If Lea was lucky, she would be able to sneak into the chaos unnoticed. She tucked her head under her wrap, slipped off her sandals, and entered her family's villa.

"Lea," her mother's voice sounded from above.

She froze.

Her mother, Kelilah, stood at the top of the staircase. Her broad hips and plump face revealed to the world she had borne her fair share of children and enjoyed the pleasures of rich society.

"Where have you been?" she asked as she hurried down the steps.

"I got caught up in the shops."

Her mother stopped a few steps shy of the bottom. "You were wasting your time at the bay again, weren't you?"

She bowed her head. "Yes, Ima."

"I've told you not to waste your time dreaming about faraway lands when your work is here." She waved around the large room. "Now, get those supplies into the kitchen." She turned and rushed back upstairs.

"Yes, Ima."

Lea slipped the wrapped gift from her bag before she willingly deposited the rest into the hands of neighbor women and family members who were helping with the preparations.

In her room, she placed the gift under her pillow until time would bring her sister's bridegroom to retrieve his bride. She looked around the chamber she had shared with her three older sisters.

Her oldest sister, Zahara, had been married for years and made Lea an aunt twice over already. Jerusha, the next in line, wasted no time in begging Abba to arrange her marriage as soon as she was old enough. Nava, the third sister, had waited a bit longer, but any day would be the last she would reside under their shared roof. When the bridegroom comes, Lea would be the last sister left unmarried at the age of nineteen.

She sat on the edge of Nava's bed and sniffled. The warring emotions of sorrow and joy battled for release. She was happy for her sister. Daniel was a good man who feared Yahweh. In fact, all her sisters married good men. Abba had seen well to those arrangements. But what was to become of her?

"Ima said you'd be in here."

Lea lifted her damp eyes to see Zahara leaning against the doorpost. Childbearing and rearing had not marred her sister's beauty one bit. She still looked as though she had come from a full day of Roman beauty treatments. Her hair was carefully pinned to tame it and her face was painted with simple embellishments.

"Ima also said you spent the morning down at the bay again."

Lea let her gaze drop to the majestic mosaic lion embedded into the floor.

"You shouldn't spend so much time there alone. It's dangerous." Zahara sat on the bed beside her. "Slave traders could snatch you away and sell you to the highest bidder. Or toss you on one of their ships and take you away from us."

Lea scoffed at her sister's fear. No one wanted her. That was part of the problem.

"Do you remember when we used to imagine this lion would take us away?"

Zahara glanced at the floor and smiled. "You

were the one always imagining."

"I still want to see wild lions. Not like the ones in the arena that are beaten and chained, but ones roaming free."

Zahara stroked Lea's head. "Always dreaming of far off lands."

"You sound like Ima."

"Well, I am one you know." She winked.

"Where are my nephews?"

"I'm sure they are running under the feet of the ladies in the kitchen. They're hoping someone will give them a treat."

"I should make myself useful by entertaining them. These days of waiting must be so boring for two young boys." She rose.

"Why do you spend your time by the bay anyway?"

Lea stopped at the door. "The salt air tastes like freedom."

"Is your life here so strangling that you would risk enslavement to be rid of it?"

"That's just it." Lea looked over her shoulder. "I don't know what lies ahead of me. But something out there calls me."

"Yahweh has called you to be here until Abba has arranged for your future."

"What if Yahweh is the one calling me out there, while Abba's will is that I remain here?"

Zahara stood. "You believe Yahweh has called

you away?"

"Yes. No. I don't know." She shook her head as if trying to clear the fog of thoughts and dreams.

"Then I strongly suggest you stay in your place and allow Abba to guide you to what Yahweh has for you."

"And if my place is out there somewhere?"

Zahara sighed. "Then trust that Abba will listen to Him."

Lea found her two nephews in the kitchen as her sister suggested. They were nibbling on some goat cheese under a table.

"Come boys," she called to them. "Sit in the courtyard with me and I'll tell you a story."

The two boys scurried from their place.

One of the women gave Lea a grateful look before returning to her chopping.

Lea walked along the pebbled path which led up the center of the courtyard. She saw the boys hiding among the shrubs.

She sat on a nearby bench. "And where have my nephews gone?" She laid a hand to her brow and pretended to search for them. "I suppose I shall have to tell myself a story."

"Here we are!" Aaron popped his head out of a bush.

Little Isaiah crawled out from under the branches and climbed onto the bench beside her. "We want to hear the story."

Lea plucked a stray twig from his hair. "And which would you like to hear?"

"Tell us the one about the great fish," Aaron suggested.

"No, no. Tell us the one about the frogs," the younger brother pleaded.

"How about the one with the lions." He curled his fingers and growled.

"That one's too scary." Isaiah tucked his head under Lea's arm.

"I like scary." He roared his best roar.

Lea thought for a moment. "How about the one with Ruth?"

"That's a girl story," Aaron protested. "I want to hear about an adventure."

"Ruth did go on an adventure. Don't you remember?"

Aaron climbed out of the shrub and folded his arms over his chest. "A *real* adventure."

"What about David?" Isaiah offered.

"Yes, tell us about David."

"David's life was filled with many adventures. Which one shall we hear today?"

"The one with the giant." Aaron lifted himself onto his tiptoes and reached above his head.

Isaiah nodded vigorously.

"There once was a shepherd boy named David," Lea started and brushed some loose leaves from her lap. "He was the youngest of eight brothers. He was small, but Yahweh had already told him he was going to be a mighty king.

"One day, he visited his brothers in the valley of Elah where the Israelites were fighting the Philistines. David heard one Philistine, a giant by the name of Goliath, taunt the Israelites by saying—"

"I defy the ranks of Israel this day." Aaron picked up a long branch and held it high. "Give me a man that we may fight together."

Lea chuckled. "This happened for forty days until David asked…" She nudged Isaiah.

He hopped off the bench and stood beside his older brother. "Who is this uncircumcised Philistine that he should defy the armies of the living God?"

"The soldiers told King Saul what David had said. And David told Saul…" Lea nodded to her young nephew.

"Let no man's heart fail because of him. Your servant will go and fight this Philistine."

"But Saul told David he was too young to battle the giant. Goliath had been in war since he was a young boy. David was only a shepherd," Lea explained. "But David told Saul…"

Isaiah smiled. "It's true that I am only a shepherd boy, but Yahweh has delivered me from the paw of the lion and from the paw of the bear. He will deliver me from the hand of this Philistine too."

"King Saul put his royal armor on little David, but it was so heavy that David couldn't move. So, he took it off. Instead of the armor, David went down to a nearby stream and collected five smooth stones." She held up her fingers. "With his sling in his hand, he went back to the valley to face Goliath. And the giant said…"

"Am I a dog that you come at me with sticks?" Aaron asked.

"David said…" Lea pointed to Isaiah.

"You come to me with a spear and javelin, but I come to you in the name of Yahweh, the God of the armies of Israel, who you have defied. He will deliver you into my hands and will give your flesh to the birds of the field. Then all the earth will know that there is a God in Israel."

"So, David drew out one of the stones from his shepherd's pouch," Lea continued, "and slung it at Goliath."

Isaiah pretended to load his imaginary sling and tossed a stone in Aaron's direction.

"And the stone struck Goliath in his forehead and he fell on his face."

Aaron imitated being struck and made gurgling sounds as he fell forward.

Lea giggled. "David didn't have a sword, so he ran over to Goliath and drew his sword out of its sheath."

Isaiah strolled over to his brother and picked up the branch. He raised it high.

"Then he cut off the head of the giant."

The younger brother brought the fake sword down on Aaron's neck.

"When the other Philistines saw their champion was dead, they ran away in fear," Lea finished.

Isaiah jumped around in victory. "Praise Yahweh!"

Aaron rose from the ground. "Now *that* was a story."

"I'm so glad you enjoyed it."

"I'm going to be brave like David one day." Isaiah spun the stick in his hand.

She hugged her youngest nephew close. "David was brave because Yahweh had given him experience. He didn't live his life knowing he was going to face Goliath. He followed Yahweh each day."

"I'm going to fight lions like David," Aaron boasted.

"You can't fight any lions," Isaiah protested. "You're not a gladiator."

"I could if I wanted to."

"Nuh-uh."

"Can too."

"Enough," Lea corrected. "Aaron, you shouldn't want to fight like the gladiators. They risk their lives for entertainment."

"But they are so strong and brave. I do want to be like them."

"Why not be like David and follow Yahweh?"

"Do you think He'd ever call me to fight a giant?"

"Only He knows His plans for you."

"Tell us another story," Isaiah begged.

The distant sound of a shofar echoed around them.

"I'm afraid it's time for us to get ready." Lea ruffled her nephew's hair.

"Aww, I wanted to hear another one of your stories."

"How about this," Lea offered, "if you behave yourselves at the feast, I'll ask your mother if I can put you to bed tonight and I'll tell you another."

"Promise?"

"Promise." She smiled and watched the two boys run into the house.

Inside her empty room, Lea retrieved her hidden gift and picked up her brass mirror to check her hair. Some pieces had fallen out of place.

"Can I help with that?" Jerusha, her second oldest sister, came up behind her.

Lea nodded.

"It's gotten so long since the last time I helped you." She ran her fingers through Lea's dark strands.

"I need something to attract men. At least that's what Ima says."

Jerusha pinned the few loose bits. "You know she means well."

"I wish her words were sweeter."

"She does love you. Her and Abba both simply want the best for you."

"I know that too."

She tucked another section into a pin. "How's it feel to finally have this room all to yourself?"

"Lonely."

Jerusha stopped. "I didn't mean…"

Lea patted her hand. "I know." She hugged her sister. "I am happy for each of you. I'd want nothing more than all the happiness in the world for my sisters. But somedays I feel as if I'm left to an unknown path."

"Yahweh will guide your path."

"Then why hasn't He yet?"

She twisted a pin in her hand. "How do you know He hasn't?"

"I don't."

"Then have a little faith. Your time will come, sweet sister." She kissed her forehead.

"I suppose."

"Now, let's get downstairs before they leave without us."

Lea joined the large processional from their house to the synagogue where their father, Rabbi

Caleb, blessed the union.

Nava, Lea's third oldest sister, sat next to her bridegroom, Daniel. She couldn't take her eyes off him. Lea could see the warmness in her sister's cheeks even under her sheer veil.

When the ceremony was complete, Daniel took Nava away to the home he had purchased for them. After a short time, they returned to take their honored place among their guests to signal the start of the wedding feast.

After helping Zahara gather food for her two boys, Lea stole away to congratulate the couple. "May Yahweh bless you," she bowed to Daniel.

"Greetings, new sister." He bowed back. "I'm so happy you could share this day with us."

"I would be found no other place, dear brother." She knelt beside her sister. "I have a gift for your wedding day."

Nava's eyes brightened. "Really?"

She opened her bag and retrieved the gift. "This is for you."

Nava carefully unwrapped the fabric to reveal a polished silver salt shaker. It practically glowed in the lamplight.

"Oh, sister. It's beautiful." She pulled Lea in close and embraced her.

"I'd been saving for months. Do you truly like it?"

A tear streamed down her cheek. "I do. It's the

most precious gift of the night."

"That's where you're wrong, my love," Daniel interrupted. "You are." He winked.

Nava's blush grew wider.

"I shall leave you two to your other guests."

"Thank you, sister." Nava pulled her in for another hug. "I shall treasure it always."

She rose and made her way back to her nephews. "Are we ready?"

Zahara lifted an eyebrow.

"I promised the boys I'd put them to bed tonight so we could share another story."

"But don't you want to stay?"

"You enjoy the feast. Stay as long as you'd like. I'll sit at your house until you and Noam come home."

"You're sure?"

She nodded.

"If that is your wish."

The boys each took one of Lea's hands and led her away.

"What story will it be?" Aaron wondered as they walked the nearly empty marble-paved road.

"Tell us about Adam and Eve," Isaiah suggested.

"No, about Abba Abraham."

"How about the fall of Jericho?" Lea offered.

"Oh yes, I like that one," the younger brother agreed.

"Very well." She cleared her throat. "Once there was a woman named Rahab who lived in the city of Jericho."

Chapter Two

"And a certain Jew named Apollos, born at Alexandria, an eloquent man, and mighty in the scriptures, came to Ephesus." -Acts 18:24

The next morning shone bright on Lea's face, but her heart was clouded by emptiness. She had stayed late at Zahara's house until she was relieved of her child watching duties. Upon her return home, she spent the rest of the night tossing upon her bed. The quiet house was amplified with everyone's return to their own homes and the last sister gone from their shared room. She missed the sound of peaceful breathing beside her. When the first rays of sunlight shone through the house, Lea rose and fled to the call of the port.

Life had gone on as it always had. Ships still came and went. Merchants still set out their goods in the Agora in hopes of making a profit. The people of Ephesus carried on as though nothing had changed, but everything was different for Lea.

The sea air didn't brighten her spirit as it once did. Watching people move about their day no longer brought curiosity but sorrow. Did life have nothing more to offer her but to witness everyone else live theirs?

A heavy wind kicked up across the water and nearly pressed Lea backward. Her bag jostled against her side and caused the coins inside to jingle. She thought perhaps a stroll through the Agora would be enough of a distraction before she had to return home.

It was early enough to catch the prize offerings of the merchants. Some were still in the process of setting up their stalls as she passed by. Men called to her to stop and look at their precious stones and metals. Spices from the far reaches of the world were heaped in piles on wooden tables ready to be weighed out. Their aromas filled the fresh air. The scent of freshly baked bread called to her. She exchanged a single coin for a small loaf she nibbled on as she continued her aimless path. Flowers hung from poles, drying in the warmth of the day.

Her eyes caught the long channel through the tall pillars and she once again longed to set sail to somewhere far away.

"Greetings," a female voice interrupted her thoughts.

Lea looked at the next booth over to see a woman smiling at her. It only took a moment for her to place the seller. She was the same woman Lea had seen come into port the morning before. Her warm eyes beckoned Lea closer.

"Greetings to you." Lea moved to stand in front of the simple setup.

The woman stood on a wooden box tying a cover to one of the pillars to create a shield from the sun. "Is it your custom to stand by the bay every morning?"

Lea lifted an eyebrow.

The woman chuckled. "I remember seeing you yesterday." She hopped off the box.

"Where have you come from?"

"Corinth." She shuffled through a small pile of red deerskin that lay on her long table. "Though my husband and I were born in Rome."

Lea inwardly prided herself on guessing as much when she first laid eyes on them. All her years of people watching had served well at her private game.

The woman tilted her head.

"Forgive me." She blushed. "I'm called Lea. Welcome to Ephesus."

"It's nice to meet you, Lea. I'm called Priscilla."

A man came up behind Priscilla and dumped a pile of freshly processed leather on the table. Lea could still smell the mixture of sesame oil and alum.

"That should be the last of it," he informed Priscilla.

"Lea, I'd like you to meet my husband,

Aquila."

The man bowed. "Greetings."

"Greetings."

"Lea here was just welcoming us to her fair city."

Aquila glanced around the market. "It reminds me so much of home." He set to work straightening out his pile.

"There was a third with you," Lea wondered aloud. "Where is he?"

A knowing smile spread across Priscilla's face. "Our companion's name is Paul. He has gone on to Jerusalem to keep the feast, but we expect his return soon."

"Is he a traveling Rabbi?"

Aquila paused and glanced at his wife.

"More or less," Pricilla answered.

"Will he be teaching in the synagogue?"

"That's the plan," Aquila offered.

"Will you be staying long in Ephesus?"

It was Priscilla's turn to exchange a conferring glimpse with her husband. "We will be here until Yahweh moves us."

"You have many questions." Aquila's voice reminded Lea of her father's.

"I've been accused of such on a number of occasions."

The couple laughed together.

Lea couldn't help but be raptured in their

contagious joy. She found the sorrow of her heart lifted and even allowed herself to smile for the first time since she had put her nephews to bed the night before.

"I'm glad you've come to Ephesus."

"I am as well." Priscilla reached out her hand and placed it on Lea's.

The warm touch reassured Lea more than her words.

"I must get home now."

"We shall see you again," Priscilla promised.

A few days later, Lea accompanied her mother and father to the synagogue.

"We've got another visiting teacher today," Rabbi Caleb commented.

"Another?" Lea asked.

"Yes." Her father straightened his graying beard. "We had a fellow asked to speak, but he didn't stay. Seems he had some business in Jerusalem. Promised he'd return if he could."

"What was his name?" Kelilah adjusted her headwrap as they neared the holy building.

"Paul, I believe."

Lea perked up at the name. "Who will we hear today?"

"I believe his name is Apollos. He comes from

Alexandria, I think."

Caleb led his family through the doorway of the rectangular building. The simple room had provided years of instruction for Lea. It was here she listened to her father's voice as he led their people in the ways of Yahweh. Lining three of the four walls were steps going down to the main floor. These provided seating for the audience. A raised platform stood in the center containing a simple bench for the teacher to sit. Behind it on the empty wall stood a table with a chest which held the holy scrolls owned by Rabbi Caleb.

Lea and Kelilah took their usual seat on one of the mid-level steps to the left side of the platform.

"Rabbi Caleb, we are ready," a fellow Jew reported.

"We shall begin with a song." Caleb led those gathered in a simple song of David's and allowed the ten accounted for to recite the traditional prayers. After reading a selection from his scrolls, Rabbi Caleb announced, "We have a guest with us today." He stepped down from the raised platform and motioned a man forward.

"My name is Apollos," the man shared as he took his place in front of the crowd. "I'm grateful to Rabbi Caleb for allowing me to speak to you all today."

Caleb nodded graciously and took a seat next

to his wife.

"I've come to your city to share with you about Jesus. No doubt you've heard of the works He has done and the miracles performed in His name."

Many of the men gathered on the levels of steps muttered their agreements.

"I've come to tell you more about Him and ask that you repent and be baptized."

"Why must we?" An older man asked. "Only those outside of our fold are in need of baptism."

"Because it is what John has taught us."

"The scrolls do not teach us that such a thing is required."

"That's true."

"Then why should we conform to your request? It sounds like the path Antiochus IV tried to take by changing who we are as a people."

"I'm not asking you not to be Jewish anymore. Jesus didn't come to destroy the law, but to fulfill it. I'm asking that you repent of your ways—"

"Change what we do?"

"Only that you turn from your wicked ways and follow the path Jesus set out for us."

"You're not the first to share with us about the Way."

"It's not just about knowing the teachings, but about walking in them."

Lea's attention wavered. She didn't like the argumentative questioning the men seemed to enjoy. They often played with new teachers like a street cat toying with a rat. Her gaze searched the faces of those gathered in the room. Among the same ones she had seen since she could remember, and the mix of strangers visiting with the tide, two stood out to her from across the room. Priscilla smiled wide. Aquila nodded with recognition.

Her heart warmed at their presence.

When the meeting was complete, Lea pressed her way through the crowd to where Priscilla had sat, but they were already speaking with the guest.

"You are mighty in the Scriptures," Aquila encouraged. "Have you been taught in the Way of the Lord?"

"I have."

"Then why do you only teach the Baptism of John?"

"What other baptism is there?"

"Why don't you join us at our home?" Priscilla offered. "I can share with you."

Apollos considered the proposal for a long time before answering, "Thank you for the hospitality. I would be most grateful."

Lea tugged at Priscilla's sleeve. "You mean to instruct him?"

"Yes."

She opened her mouth to speak, but thought better and closed it.

"You have an argument as to why I shouldn't?"

"I just don't know many Jewish men who would sit at the feet of a woman."

"I've spent years under Paul's instruction. The Lord has given us much wisdom concerning Jesus as Messiah. My intent is to pass along those teachings as any good teacher would."

Priscilla's strange claim and her absolute conviction warred inside Lea's mind.

"Would you like to join us?"

"I don't know if I should."

"Why don't you ask your parents?"

Lea passed through the thinning crowd to her mother's side. "May I visit with a friend today?"

Kelilah searched the group on raised feet and with a hopeful gaze. "Who?"

She pointed to the couple waiting with Apollos. "Priscilla and Aquila are new to Ephesus. I met them in the market place. They're tentmakers."

"Oh." Kelilah dropped down. "Very well. Be home before the evening meal."

"I will."

Lea returned to Priscilla who was waiting with her husband and their other guest.

"Apollos, I'd like you to meet our friend, Lea."

"Lea bat-Caleb." She bowed.

"As in Rabbi Caleb's daughter?"

"One of them." She waited for them to get her joke, but they didn't. "I'm the youngest of four sisters."

"No wonder your father's hair is so gray." Apollos' smile lit up his eyes.

Lea laughed in spite of herself. "Abba said it's partly due to my sisters and partly due to his people."

"That I can understand," Apollos sympathized. "People are not the easiest things to lead."

They spoke of simple ideas until they reached a small house.

"Here we are," Priscilla announced.

"It's not much, but it's comfortable," Aquila added. "We are renting it for now and share the courtyard with some lovely families."

The mid-day meal was spread before them and Aquila took the honor of blessing the food.

"As we spoke briefly in the synagogue," Priscilla recalled. "We wish to explain to you the baptism of the Holy Spirit."

Apollos' eyes widened.

"You see, the Baptism of John was where Jesus' ministry started, but not where it stopped. Jesus promised when he left that another would come."

"And how do we know when the other comes?"

"He already came," Aquila explained.

"On the day of Pentecost after Jesus had ascended," Priscilla started. "His disciples were gathered together in one place. Suddenly, a sound came from heaven like a rushing wind. It filled the entire house. Over each one of them appeared cloven tongues like fire. They were filled with the Holy Spirit and began speaking in other languages.

"The Feast had brought Jews from all over the world to Jerusalem. These men heard the disciples speaking in their own language about the works of God. This confused them because they recognized the disciples were from Galilee and not intelligent men. Some of them mocked the disciples by claiming they were drunk. That's when Peter stepped in and explained to those listening that they were not drunk because it was only the third hour of the day.

"Peter told them the prophet Joel had spoken about these things. He told them that God would pour out His Spirit on them. That is the baptism we teach."

"And what of John's Baptism?"

"John taught one should repent and be prepared for what was coming. Jesus came and when He left, the Holy Spirit came to baptize us as Joel spoke. John was pointing to the coming Messiah."

"Jesus."

"Exactly."

Apollos pondered on the words. "Thank you

for sharing with me. I understand much better now."

"Are you staying in Ephesus?" Lea asked.

"Actually, I'm inclined to move on to the province of Achaia."

"We are from Corinth and know many of the believers there," Priscilla explained.

"Would they receive me well?"

"We shall write a letter of commendation for you," Aquila offered.

"Oh, yes," his wife agreed. "That is an excellent idea."

"You are most kind."

Lea watched as another path was laid before someone else. She felt a pinch of jealousy in her heart as a faraway journey was about to start for her new friend, Apollos. She wondered when the time would come to start her own journey.

Chapter Three

"Paul came also to Derbe and to Lystra. A disciple was there, named Timothy, the son of a Jewish woman who was a believer, but his father was a Greek." -Acts 16:1

"Is Paul speaking again today?" Lea asked her father as they prepared to leave their home.

"How long has it been now?" her mother wondered as she chose a cloth to cover her hair.

"Coming up on three months," Rabbi Caleb answered. "I will allow him to speak as long as he doesn't cause trouble like he has other places."

"Has he really done the things they claim he has?"

"All I know is the Jews here have accepted him and have been attentive to his teaching." He lifted a bushy brow. "So far."

Lea clearly caught the warning in her father's voice.

"I hear he is staying with your tent making friends," Kelilah commented.

"He is. I haven't had a chance to meet him yet." An idea struck her. "May I have permission to join them today after the meeting?"

"If they invite you, you may," Rabbi Caleb answered.

Lea walked the familiar path toward the synagogue with a light heart hoping to spend the rest of the day with Priscilla.

She and her mother took their customary spot.

Rabbi Caleb started the meeting with their traditions before inviting Paul to speak.

Lea easily found Priscilla and Aquila in their usual seat. Next to Aquila sat a young man that she had never seen before. Though visitors were common in their port city, the man seemed to sit closer to the couple than a stranger.

After Paul taught and the members were dismissed to enjoy the rest of their day in fellowship, Lea stole away to her favorite couple.

"Lea, how nice to see you," Priscilla greeted her warmly.

"And you."

"I'd like you to meet our friend, Timothy."

The young man next to Aquila bowed with a broad smile.

"Timothy, this is our Ephesian hostess, Lea. She's the daughter of Rabbi Caleb."

"Greetings." He bowed respectfully. "I enjoyed your father's leadership today."

Lea's heart pounded at the sound of his voice. "We are the ones honored by your visit. Will you be in Ephesus long?"

She didn't think it was possible for his grin to get any wider, but it did.

"I…," he fumbled.

"Timothy here was going to join us today to regale us with his recent travels," Priscilla intervened. "Would you like to join us, Lea?"

She felt warmth creep into her cheeks and could only nod.

"Then it's settled. Shall we go?" She took her husband's elbow and headed for the door.

Priscilla served the group in their modest rented home not far from the synagogue. Paul joined them while they ate.

"Paul," Priscilla handed him a cup, "this is Rabbi Caleb's daughter, Lea."

"Welcome, young one." He nodded his head to her. Lea noticed his hair had begun to grow again. "Your father is a well-respected man here. It's an honor to be able to teach for so long to our people."

"We are happy to have you."

"Timothy, why don't you tell Lea how you met Paul," Priscilla offered.

Timothy faced Lea across the table. "A few years ago, Paul came to my home town of Lystra. He was teaching through the area, I heard the message of the Way, and decided to follow."

"Didn't your family have a problem with you

leaving our traditions?"

"I'm only half Jewish. My father is Greek. My mother, a Jewess. She and my Safta Lois taught me about Yahweh, but my father didn't allow them to let me be fully Jewish."

"Meaning?"

"Meaning we had to get my boy here," Paul slapped Timothy on the shoulder, "circumcised when he was in his nineteenth year."

Timothy's cheeks shaded crimson.

"I see." Lea glanced down at her drink.

"I would have done anything to teach and understood why it needed to be done."

"And I couldn't pass up someone whose name had been on the lips of fellow believers all the way to Iconium," Paul explained.

"Then what happened?" Lea asked.

"I witnessed Paul endure many things as we traveled. We went through Phrygia and Galatia. We attempted to go further east, but the Holy Spirit forbade us. So, we went west to Troas and met up with Paul's physician companion, Luke. That night Paul had a vision." He looked at his mentor.

"A man from Macedonia stood by me pleading that I come to help them."

"Did you?" she wondered.

"We headed out the next morning for Samothrace and Neapolis," Timothy answered.

"From there, we stopped in Philippi for a few days to preach to a Roman colony. When we went down to the river on the Sabbath, some women were there praying. We spoke to them about the Way. One of them, a woman named Lydia, understood Paul's preaching and was baptized right there in the river."

Lea enjoyed the way his eyes glistened when he spoke of the moment.

"She went back into the city and brought her entire household with her begging Paul to baptize them all. She was so grateful that she practically forced us to stay with her."

Paul chuckled. "Lydia is a very persuasive woman."

"What happened after that?"

Timothy and Paul exchanged a silent glance.

"Keep going, son. I'm not ashamed of where the Lord has led me."

"We were heading to a house of prayer when we came upon a woman who was possessed."

"Possessed?" Lea placed a hand over her heart. "The poor thing."

"She was kept that way because the spirit in her could speak things about the future. Her masters were making a lot of money off her abilities. She followed us yelling, 'These men are servants of the Most High God, who proclaim to you the way of salvation.' She did this for many days. After a while, Paul got tired of her and commanded the spirit to leave her in the name of Jesus."

"Did it?"

"Yes, but her masters were not happy. They laid hands on Paul and Silas and dragged them to the marketplace in front of the magistrates. They accused them of stirring up trouble by teaching customs against Roman beliefs. When the judges heard the accusations, they ripped their clothes and ordered Paul and Silas to be beaten."

Paul rubbed his shoulder.

"A lashing wasn't good enough for those bloodthirsty Romans," Timothy continued. "So, they threw them in prison. The guard who was placed over them moved them into the inner prison and put their feet in stocks."

"How awful."

"Perhaps he had heard how Peter had walked out of not one but two prisons with the help of a few angels," Paul joked.

"When did they finally let you go?" Lea questioned.

"After Yahweh showed them who was really in charge."

"Another angel escape?"

Paul laughed and wiped away a tear. "No, but just as dramatic. At midnight, Silas and I were praying and singing Yahweh's praises."

"What they didn't know was Luke and I had

been praying all evening and night with Lydia and many other believers," Timothy explained.

Paul patted his younger companion's arm before continuing, "A great earthquake shook the foundations of the prison causing all the doors and our chains to open."

"So that's how you escaped?"

"Not exactly."

Lea raised an eyebrow.

"The guard was stirred from his slumber. When he saw all the doors open, he took out his sword and was going to kill himself."

"Oh my!" She covered her mouth.

"His superiors would have done it for him if they discovered all the prisoners gone on his watch. But I told him not to harm himself because we were all there and accounted for. He called for a torch so he could see for himself. When he saw that we truly were still there, he knelt at our feet and asked us what he must do to be saved."

"Really?" She smiled despite herself.

Paul nodded. "We told him to believe on the Lord Jesus Christ."

"That simple?"

"That simple. We explained to him about the word of the Lord."

"That's amazing."

"That's not the best part," Timothy added. "The guard took Paul and Silas and washed and bound their wounds. Then he took them home and fed them while they talked to his entire household about Jesus."

"In the middle of the night?"

"I take any opportunity I'm given," Paul answered. "We even baptized them because they all believed our words."

"Was the guard able to secure your release then?"

"No." He shook his head. "The guard eventually had to return us to the prison. But come daylight, the same ones who had beaten us with rods showed up at the jail with word of our release from the magistrates."

"Good."

"Paul didn't take it," Timothy said.

"You didn't?"

"They had accused and beaten us publicly and then they simply wanted to alleviate their conscience privately. I wasn't going to have it."

"What did you do?"

"He sent those officials back with a message," Timothy responded.

"A message?"

"If they wanted us freed, they could come get us themselves." Paul emphasized his words with a swift nod of his head.

Lea laughed. "You did not do such a thing."

"I did."

"He also revealed to them they had imprisoned a couple of Roman citizens," Timothy added.

"What did they do?"

"They came to free us and begged that we not turn them in for illegal imprisonment."

"You should have." Timothy folded his arms across his chest.

"I had half a mind too, but it wasn't the Lord's will."

"We sure were surprised when they walked into Lydia's house that day. The group there loved on them while they shared the story. We spent much of the day praying and praising Yahweh."

"And then?" Lea asked.

"Luke decided to stay in Philippi, but the rest of us headed on to Amphipolis and Apollonia. Finally, we came to Thessalonica. Paul preached in their synagogue first like he did wherever there was one."

"Did you see many come to the Way?"

"Oh yes. Even some of the prominent women. But the Jews in the city didn't like us teaching about Jesus. They stirred up a crowd to accuse us of acting against the decrees of Caesar and claiming Jesus was another king instead of Caesar. They ambushed a believer's house trying to find us. Grabbed poor Jason and took him to the city officials."

"What did they do?"

"They made Jason and many of the other believers pay a fine. But then they let them go."

"Well at least they didn't end up in prison."

"After that, the believers were not too happy with us. They asked us to leave and so we headed to Berea. The people there were much more willing to hear the message. But it didn't take long before the people from Thessalonica came to town to stir up trouble again."

"What did you do?"

"I told Timothy and Silas to stay there while I headed on to Athens," Paul replied.

"Silas and I encouraged the believers in Thessalonica," Timothy explained. "Until we later met Paul in Corinth."

Lea turned to Priscilla. "That's where you met Paul?"

She smiled. "Yahweh had arranged our meeting. We also got to know young Timothy as well."

He beamed at her. "I helped encourage the house church they started in Corinth and also traveled back and forth to Thessalonica."

"I know that the three of them came here to Ephesus," Lea remembered. "But you weren't among them when they arrived."

"Silas wanted to stay longer, so I remained with him going back and forth between Corinth and Thessalonica until I received word that Paul had settled here in Ephesus."

"We just sent a man named Apollos to Corinth with a letter of recommendation," Priscilla said.

"I'm happy to hear the church there will continue to be encouraged."

Timothy rose to help Aquila and Priscilla clear the empty platters.

Tears streamed down Lea's cheeks as she sat alone at the table with Paul.

"What's wrong, young one?" Paul reached for her hand.

"My heart is pricked like Lydia and your Philippian guard." She wiped her face on her sleeve. "Hearing everything Yahweh has done and listening to you preach in the synagogue these past few months has opened me to your message. I too want to know what I must do to be saved."

"I've preached the same message since I encountered the resurrected Jesus on the road to Damascus. You must believe in the Lord Jesus to be saved."

"I do," she sobbed. "I believe Jesus is the Messiah we've been longing for."

"Then I shall baptize you myself right now." Paul rose and announced to the group, "Lea has believed on Jesus. We shall take her to be baptized."

They rejoiced with her and left at once out of the city and along the wall until it opened into the channel.

Lea slipped off her sandals and left her headwrap behind before she waded into the Cayster River with Paul until the water came up above her midsection.

"Lea bat-Caleb, do you believe Jesus is Messiah?" Paul's voice boomed over the water.

"I do."

"Do you believe He was crucified, buried, and on the third day rose again to secure for us the resurrection of the dead?"

"I do."

"Then I baptize you, my sister, in the name of Jesus."

Lea closed her eyes while Paul dipped her into the water and helped her rise again. When her face broke the surface, she could hear the group shouting from the shore.

She attempted to sprint toward them, but the water slowed her down.

Aquila and Timothy sung a song.

Priscilla had a blanket ready to wrap around her along with an earnest embrace when her toes touched the sand.

"I'm so happy for you," the older woman whispered in her ear.

When the men's song was complete, Paul put his hand on Lea's shoulder. "Jesus, I ask that You pour out Your Holy Spirit on our new sister."

Lasting Legacy

Water dripped from everywhere on Lea, but a warmth spread through her from the inside out.

Paul's prayer flowed over her like a soft wave and she nearly cried from the joy that ignited in her soul.

Chapter Four

"And God wrought special miracles by the hands of Paul: So that from his body were brought unto the sick handkerchiefs or aprons, and the diseases departed from them, and the evil spirits went out of them." -Acts 19:11-12

The following Sabbath, Lea took her place next to her mother in the synagogue. She tried to avert her eyes from the young man who sat with Priscilla, but found it difficult to concentrate on anything else. His warm smile was like a fireside she never wanted to leave.

"Who is that man sitting with your friends?" Kelilah questioned. "I saw him last week as well."

Lea forced her gaze to her folded hands. "His name is Timothy. He's from Lystra, but he has been traveling all over Macedonia and Achaia helping Paul with his ministry." She dared another peek at him attempting to cover her desire not to turn away.

As if he heard her speak, Timothy looked their way and bowed his head.

"Is he a Jew?"

Lea groped for words. Timothy was only half Jew by birth, but all Jew by tradition. She wanted her mother to see him in the best possible light. "Yes. His mother and grandmother practice our traditions and still live in Lystra."

"And his father?"

She chided herself for divulging information beyond a simple answer, but she knew better than to try to hide anything from her mother. The synagogue leader's wife had ears everywhere. "His father is Greek."

Kelilah turned her whole body toward her daughter with a furrowed brow.

"But," Lea continued in hopes of stomping out any prejudice her mother may be forming before even meeting the man. "Timothy has chosen to live out the traditions of the Jewish lifestyle since becoming a man."

"I see."

"Where are Zahara and Noam?" Lea grasped for another topic. "I didn't see them come in."

Kelilah craned her neck in search of her eldest daughter. "She is not among us. We shall visit her after the meeting."

"I do hope all is well."

Rabbi Caleb stepped forward to signal the start of the meeting. After songs and prayers, Paul was once again invited to speak.

As he spoke, the words fell new on Lea.

Though she had given her undivided attention to Paul's teaching for the last three months, this morning's lesson was like fresh wind in her sails. The things that he taught about the kingdom of Yahweh pieced together in her mind like never before.

"Why do you continue teaching such nonsense?" a man's voice from the front interrupted Paul's words.

Lea recognized him as a prominent man by the name of Gedaliah.

"I testify of the truth," Paul urged.

"Truth." He grunted. "You and your Way followers spread falseness."

"Brother, I can assure you I speak only that which is true."

"You've been babbling on for months and have yet to persuade any of us of your Way."

Paul glanced to his group sitting together and then let a quick glance fall on Lea before turning back to the man.

"You wish to rid the world of Jews," Gedaliah argued on. "There have been many like you before, but Yahweh has preserved us."

"I mean no harm to anyone."

He rose from his seat and wagged his finger at Paul. "You won't be happy until you turn all of us away from our heritage."

"I'm here to speak of Jesus and Him crucified

and resurrected—"

He covered his ears and rocked back and forth. "Lies!"

Many other men shouted.

Rabbi Caleb stood and tried to calm them, but the men continued their uproar. Finally, he spoke something in Paul's ear and waved his hand toward the door.

Paul motioned for his group to follow him.

Lea wanted to follow too, but her mother grabbed her arm.

"Stay put until this crowd settles. You don't want to be caught in their siege."

She searched her mother's face hoping for any give in the order, but she found none. "Yes, Ima."

When the room was empty, Kelilah stood and Lea took the opportunity to seek out her father.

"What did you say to him?"

Rabbi Caleb continued putting away the scrolls. "I told him he was no longer welcome to speak in my synagogue."

"Abba, how could you?"

He paused. "I told you what I told him when he first arrived, that he was welcomed to teach as long as he didn't cause any trouble. Today was the breaking point." He closed the lid on the chest and turned to face his daughter. "It's obvious the men do not wish to hear from him any further."

"But if they would just hear what he had to

say—"

Caleb put up a hand. "They've given him longer than most. He didn't persuade them. The matter is closed."

"But Abba —"

He silenced her with a stern look. "I said the matter is closed."

"Yes, Abba." She bowed and hurried out of the synagogue.

Lea was halfway home when she remembered that her mother wouldn't be there. They had made plans to visit Zahara. She turned around in the middle of Curetes Street and hurried to her sister's home.

The air outside the door felt heavy as Lea removed her sandals. She knew something awful awaited her before she even stepped inside. The house was quiet, but not empty.

"Zahara?" Lea's voice trembled.

"Here I am," her sister called.

Lea followed her voice until she found her sitting with their mother in a side room. Zahara was crumpled in Kelilah's embrace and dabbing her eyes with a cloth.

"What's wrong?"

Zahara looked up to Kelilah to form the words she obviously couldn't bring herself to say.

"It's Isaiah."

Lea's heart nearly shattered at the mention of

her youngest nephew's name. "Where is he?"

Kelilah reached out a hand to her. "He's in his room—"

That was all Lea needed to hear before she ran out of the room. She took the stairs two at a time as she climbed to the second story where the boy's room was located.

When she cleared the doorway, she found Noam praying over his son. She quietly knelt beside him.

Her brother-in-law looked up at her and then focused on the boy. "He's so sick."

Lea surveyed her nephew. He was laying on his bed covered in sweat. His skin was as pale as a dead body. His eyes were closed and his breathing was labored.

"How long has he been like this?" she asked as tears streamed down her face.

"Days."

She reached for the rag in a nearby bowl and rung it out. Carefully, she wiped the boy's brow. "Has a doctor come?"

"Two. They gave us things to try, but nothing has helped." Noam clasped his son's small hand in both of his and lowered his forehead to the back of his hand.

"What else can be done?"

He slowly raised his head and shook it.

"There has to be something more we can do."

"I'm doing the best thing I know how to do." He bowed his head again and whispered prayers to Yahweh.

Lea joined in with her own petitions. When she had spoken all the silent pleas she could, she looked up at the boy. As she wiped his sweat-soaked forehead, a thought took hold in her heart. "Maybe there is something else."

Noam looked up with questions in his eyes.

"I'll return as soon as I can." She rose from the bedside and hurried down the steps. As she ran from the house and to the other side of town, she prayed the man she sought would not only hear her, but intervene for her nephew.

When she found the small rented house, she pounded on the door.

"Lea?" Priscilla answered the door. "You look a fright. What's the matter?"

"Is Paul here?"

She waved her inside.

Lea realized she didn't return her sandals to her feet when she left her sister's home, so she wiped her feet as best she could and entered.

Without hesitation or guidance, she went deep into the house and found Paul speaking with another man. She recognized him as Tyrannus, a notable Greek who founded a school in their city.

"Forgive the intrusion." She bowed deeply.

Paul looked at her and then returned his

attention to his guest. "Tyrannus, this is Lea, Rabbi Caleb's daughter."

"The same Rabbi who kicked you out of his synagogue today?" Tyrannus chuckled deeply.

"The same."

Lea wrung her hands and bit her lip.

"Tyrannus and I were just discussing…" Paul started and then stopped to study Lea. "But I see there is something more pressing you'd like to discuss."

"It's my nephew. H-h-he's not well."

"Speak on, young one."

Lea took a breath. "My nephew, Isaiah, he's not well and I was hoping that you would come and pray for him."

"I understand, but I am in the middle of a meeting."

Her gaze dropped.

"But here." He held out the cloth he had in his hand. "Take this. Lay it on the child and he shall be made well in the name of Jesus."

She reached for the cloth and found her fingers trembling.

"Trust me. Your nephew will be returned to you."

She held the cloth by the corner praying that she would not contract any healing from it before returning to Isaiah. "Thank you."

He simply nodded and turned back to his

guest.

Lea rushed from the house without saying any more and hurried through the streets until she reached her sister's home.

Her toes brushed every other step as she hastened to her nephew's room.

Noam still knelt beside his son's bed in prayer.

Lea pushed passed him and spread the cloth over Isaiah's forehead.

"Where did you go?"

"To see Paul." She knelt.

"Is he a doctor?"

"No. He is a man of Yahweh."

"The traveling Pharisee who has been speaking at the synagogue?"

She nodded, but kept her eyes on the cloth.

"What did he say?"

"He gave me this cloth and told me Isaiah would be healed in the name of Jesus."

"That zealot? You believe my son will be healed in the name of a dead trouble maker?" He reached for the cloth.

Lea grabbed his arm. "Look!"

Isaiah's breathing evened out and his skin gradually darkened to his normal olive complexion.

"It's working," she whispered.

"I don't believe it."

Isaiah slowly opened his eyes. "Aunt Lea?

Abba?"

"We're here, s-s-son." Noam's voice shook.

Lea leaned over and kissed the boy's cheek. "What's going on?"

"You've been very sick," Noam explained.

"But Jesus has healed y—"

"Lea, may I have a word with you? In private." His eyes were dark and demanding. He pressed off the bed and stormed out of the room.

She rose and followed him. She turned and gave a wink over her shoulder to Isaiah. "I'll be right back," she promised. "Maybe I'll tell you a story."

He smiled wide.

When she found her brother-in-law, he was standing at the other end of the hallway with his arms folded across his broad chest.

"I meant no harm."

He held up a hand. "I know you've been spending time with that group of Way followers."

Lea felt the heat rise in her neck.

"Zahara talks to me about everything. She was concerned. I told her they seemed harmless and Abba Caleb trusted Paul enough to let him speak as long as he had. But I don't want you talking to my children about the things they teach. In this house, we follow Yahweh and only Yahweh."

"But they follow Yahweh too. Jesus is the Messiah we've been waiting for. Didn't you see the miracle that just took place in front of your own eyes?"

"So, you're starting to believe their lies? What would Abba Caleb say about that?"

"If he would listen to what they have to say—"

"What is going on up here?" Zahara stood at the top of the stairs.

"Lea and I were about to come get you. It seems Isaiah is doing better."

Zahara ducked into her son's room.

Noam looked down at Lea. "I would suggest you think long and hard about what might come from making a decision like following the Way. Your father is the most respected Jewish man in our community. You would bring great shame upon your family. Think of your mother and your sisters."

"You won't tell Abba, will you?"

"No. It's not my place."

She breathed a sigh of relief.

"But you'd better seek his wisdom sooner rather than later." He pressed past her and disappeared into the room.

Lea fought down the lump in her throat. His words were true. She hadn't thought about what following the Way would mean for her family. She had jumped headfirst into an ocean without thinking. Though the truth of the Way and what Paul taught about Jesus made the scrolls sing for the first time in her life. How could something that made her feel so close to Yahweh be the thing to drive her family apart?

She stood in the doorway of the boy's room and watched as her sister and brother-in-law took turns hugging Isaiah. They passed him back and forth between them until he protested.

"I'm hungry," his voice was weak, but pleading.

"I shall make you whatever you wish." Zahara kissed her son on the top of the head as she once again passed him into the arms of his father.

She rose and came to Lea. "Isn't it wonderful?"

Lea painted on a smile and turned to follow her sister.

"Aunt Lea, will you tell me a story now?" Isaiah's soft request carried to her.

She turned back to see Noam raise a warning eyebrow.

"How about I let you rest today and I'll stop by tomorrow to tell you a story."

He groaned.

"I think that's a good idea," his father offered. "You've been very sick and you still need some rest."

Lea stepped cautiously inside to give a farewell hug to her nephew. She was careful not to meet her brother-in-law's eyes. "I promise I will return with the sun and we shall share in many wonderful adventures with our favorite people of Yahweh."

"Like David?" His eyes shone.

"Yes." She smiled. "Like David. And I'll even tell you about your namesake, the great prophet Isaiah."

He yawned. "Tomorrow then?"

"Tomorrow." She kissed his head. Then she noticed the cloth laying behind him on the bed. She slid it into her pocket and ruffled her nephew's hair.

On her way out of the house, she promised her mother she would be home for the evening meal. Her sandals waited for her on the other side of the front door and she slipped them on.

The streets were not as crowded with the high sun. Most people retired to their cool dwellings to wait out the heat of the day. The merchant booths would be closed until later so Lea didn't have much with which to distract herself. Her father would be home alone and she wasn't ready to face him quite yet. She thought about dropping in on one of her other sisters, but wasn't in a visiting mood.

Her feet took her on a path back to a house in which she always felt welcome.

Priscilla's warm embrace was all she needed to reassure her she had chosen well.

"How's your nephew?"

Lea smiled to herself. "He became well almost

as soon as I placed Paul's cloth on him."

"Praise our Lord."

Paul entered the room.

Lea pulled his cloth out of her pocket and handed it to him. "I came to return this. In case someone else needed it."

He took the material and turned it over in his hands. "You do realize there is no power in the cloth, young one. The power comes from Jesus and His decision to heal. Sometimes He simply uses unique vessels to do His work. Your faith has healed your nephew."

"Regardless, it's your property and I wanted to see it returned."

"And the boy?"

"He was up and requesting food when I left."

"I'm thrilled to hear that."

"Why aren't you spending this Sabbath with your family?" Priscilla asked. "Especially since you now have more to thank Yahweh for?"

Lea's gaze dropped to her sandals. "I-I-I had a misunderstanding with my brother-in-law."

"Nothing that can't be set right, I hope."

"No. It's just that…" She couldn't find the words to express the battle in her soul.

"Lea." The older woman waited for her to look up. "I hope you know you are free to speak here."

"I wish that were so in my own home."

"Is that the problem?"

"Part of it." She sighed. "I tried to tell my nephew that the power of Jesus had healed him, but my brother-in-law stopped me. He said he didn't want Jesus' name to be spoken in his house, especially to his children."

"You haven't told your family about your decision?" Paul asked.

She shook her head. "It all happened so fast that I hadn't had…I hadn't made the time to talk to my parents."

Priscilla squeezed her hand. "What are you afraid of?"

"Shaming my father. He's the leader of the synagogue. The entire community honors him. If his own daughter is a Way follower…"

"But you *are* a Way follower."

"I am. I do believe Jesus is our Messiah. How can I tell them without hurting them?"

"Sit." Paul waved to a stool.

Lea obeyed.

"Now, listen to me, young one. Telling them the truth is not hurting them. You can't make them believe of course, but you would also be doing them a great disservice by not speaking the truth in love. You need to be honest."

"You're right. I'll speak with them."

"And we shall pray for them." Priscilla hugged her.

Lea closed her eyes to bask in their sincere

love. If only she felt this much acceptance and freedom from her family. Their love was present, but cool. The love that washed over her in the rented house permeated through her entire body like a warm drink on a chilly day.

Chapter Five

"After these things were ended, Paul purposed in the spirit, when he had passed through Macedonia and Achaia, to go to Jerusalem, saying, After I have been there, I must also see Rome." -Acts 19:21

A.D. 54

Beads of sweat dripped from Lea's forehead. The temperature rose steadily as the day neared its midpoint. She reached the Agora in time to see many of the merchants closing their booths for the mid-day break. She waved to Priscilla who had just thrown a cover over the table of skins.

"Where is Paul?"

"He's preparing to teach."

"Where? Abba banned him from the synagogue?"

"Tyrannus has offered the use of his school during the heat of the day when there are no sessions."

"I know the school. It's a large place. Lots of room for many to hear Paul."

"You are welcome to join us there," the older woman offered.

"My wish would be to attend every day, but Abba would probably forbid it."

"Have you spoken with him?"

She sighed. "I've begun that conversation so many times, but the words never seem to come."

"Your father would appreciate your honesty and willingness to learn."

"My father would much more appreciate my silent obedience to his will for my life."

Priscilla lifted her bag strap over her head and adjusted it across her body. She wrapped an arm around the younger woman and turned her toward the rented house. "And just what is his will for your life?"

Lea fell in step beside her. "I assume the same as his plans for my older sisters. Each were married to a man he had chosen and live to serve their husband's families."

"Then why aren't you married yet?"

"Being the fourth girl in line means a lot of hand-me-downs and little left in the change purse for a wedding feast."

Priscilla chuckled. "I can understand that, but you are in your twentieth year. Surely he has made plans for you by now."

She shrugged. "They just had the cost of my sister's wedding last year. Besides, he wouldn't inform me even if he had."

"Perhaps he is waiting for the best man possible."

"Perhaps no man is willing to step forward."

The woman's deep laugh caused them both to pause. "I don't think that's the case at all. You are bright and beautiful and the daughter of the synagogue leader. Men should be waiting in line to marry you."

Lea started to walk again. "Still. I don't think I'd like someone he would choose."

"Oh?" Priscilla followed.

"Don't misunderstand. I love my father and trust his judgment. It's just that anyone he chooses won't be…"

"Won't be Timothy."

Lea froze. She rubbed her palms over her warm cheeks.

"You've spent much more time at our place since his arrival. I see the way you two look at each other."

"It doesn't matter." She shook away the thoughts of him. "Timothy is only half Jewish by birth. In my father's eyes, he is all Greek. He'd never agree to such a union. Plus, Timothy is a…"

"A Way follower," the compassion in her voice was evident.

Lea nodded as tears formed. "If only my father understood, then it wouldn't matter that Timothy isn't a Jew."

"I think you need to speak with your father about you first. You can't keep deceiving him and hoping things will work out."

"You're right as usual." She stopped to take off her sandals at the rented house. "When we are done eating, I'll make the time to speak with him."

Priscilla opened the door. "I will pray for you."

"I'm going to need it."

"There they are." Aquila opened his arms wide. "These men will soon starve if you ladies don't spread out this delicious smelling feast soon."

Paul and Timothy were already seated at the table.

"Keep your tunic straight," Priscilla ordered. "We are here now and the food will be in your bellies in no time."

Aquila stole a kiss on his wife's cheek as she passed him.

She grabbed the nearest rag and snapped it at him. "Go sit down, you old fool."

He took his seat at the head of the table.

Lea noticed Timothy enjoying the couple's marital banter as much as she did.

A knock roused Priscilla. "Are we expecting someone else?"

"None that I know of," Aquila answered as he moved to the front door.

Lea set the platters of food on the table and took her usual seat near the end with Priscilla.

A tall man entered with Aquila. He had a large bag slung across his body. Lea could smell the salty sea air still on him. He had dark hair and eyes that seem to shine as if they had been polished. His physical features were like those of her community and he had an air of familiarity about him.

"Tychicus." Paul pulled the man in for an embrace. "When did you get in?"

"Just moments ago." He set his bag down on the table with a thud. "The men at the docks easily pointed me to the house where the famous Paul laid his head." He greeted Timothy warmly. "How are you, friend?"

"Happy to see you survived another trip across the world." Timothy jabbed his elbow into his friend's ribs.

"Tychicus is from your very own city," Priscilla whispered to Lea. "Do you know him?"

"Is he a Jew?"

"By birth, yes."

"Then I must have seen him in the synagogue at some point. Though Ephesus is a large city."

"That it is."

"Sit, sit, sit." Paul waved the man to a spot next to himself. "You must be worn from your travels. We were just about to enjoy this wonderful meal Priscilla has prepared for us."

Lasting Legacy

"I could use a good meal cooked by the hands of a lovely woman." He winked to Priscilla.

"We would enjoy news from home."

"That I have."

"Well then, Paul, get to saying the blessing so we can all have what we want," Aquila joked.

Lea stifled a laugh.

"Yahweh, we thank you for the safe arrival of our dear brother, Tychicus. We bless Your name and thank You for all the many gifts You have given by Your hand."

Aquila was the first to start scooping.

"What is your news?" Paul asked.

Priscilla passed a platter to Tychicus.

"Emperor Claudius has died."

Everyone around the table went stiff.

"You're certain?" Paul wondered.

"Quite." He took several bites. "Nero has taken his place. He is allowing Jews to return to Rome."

Paul stared at the food in front of him.

"Home." The word slipped from Priscilla's lips.

"We could go home?" Aquila put his bowl down and leaned closer to Tychicus.

"He overturned Claudius' order as soon as he took the throne."

"Home." The word escaped Priscilla's mouth once more as the shock wore off. "We can go home."

Lea's heart squeezed. What would become of her if her friends left her alone in Ephesus? She had lived a simple life before their arrival, but ever since she met them and the Jesus they preached she never imagined being apart from them. Her gaze couldn't help but travel to Timothy. Would he leave her too?

"We can start to prepare at once," Aquila announced.

"No."

All eyes turned to Paul.

"No?" Aquila asked.

"Not yet. There is still much to do. First, we need to make sure it's safe. Romans will always hold a place of hatred in their hearts for us. The door is open here in Asia for the Way and we need to take it while it's open."

"But home." Priscilla shrunk.

Paul reached out and squeezed her hand. "Soon. There is much that needs to happen."

"I also have a letter from the church at Corinth." Tychicus pulled a scroll from his bag and handed it to Paul. "It is their response to your letter."

He grabbed the letter and unrolled it. "And what news have you?" He scanned the writing.

"They are thriving, but there are some who are living against your teaching."

"We'll make plans for Timothy and Erastus to go back to Macedonia while we prepare here. Their first stop should be Corinth. I shall join them there for a journey to the church to collect funds for the poor in Jerusalem. Then I want to go to Jerusalem again and distribute the funds before we head to Rome. We can plan for Priscilla and Aquila to head to Rome ahead of us."

Lea couldn't breathe. They were leaving her. Maybe not right away, but Paul was making it clear that in the too near future they would all go. Priscilla, her rock, and Timothy, her strand of hope for the future, were about to be ripped away from her.

"Excuse me." Lea stood and fled to the courtyard.

It wasn't long before Priscilla found her crying on a bench.

The older woman sat and wrapped her arm around her.

Lea turned her damp face into the dress of her friend. "Forgive me. I must seem like a silly child."

"Why all the tears?"

She looked up into her face. "You're leaving me. You're all leaving me."

It only took a moment for the words to penetrated the older woman's heart. "Oh, I see."

Lea buried her face in the fabric again and wept.

Priscilla rocked her gently. "We were a bit insensitive, weren't we?" She brushed some hair away from Lea's face. "Forgive us. When we have a mission, we are used to planning right away. We should have considered you were at the table with us."

She wiped her face with her sleeve. "It's I who should apologize. I shouldn't expect a group of travelers to take my feelings and desires into consideration when Yahweh is calling them on. I have no right to be a stumbling block."

"Trust me. Paul would not let anyone block his path when Yahweh directs his steps."

Lea nodded.

"It will be months before we leave. Plenty of time to figure things out."

"And what about Timothy?"

She took several moments to answer. "He will probably be leaving sooner."

"And my happiness with him."

"Don't despair." She hugged her tight. "All is not lost yet."

"I wish I had your confidence."

The older woman held her out to arm's length. "Come back inside and eat with us. Then go speak with your father. Spend some time praying and seeking wisdom. Aquila and I will speak with Timothy. We will find the path Yahweh has for all of us."

"What would I ever have done without you?"

"It's a good thing neither of us has to find out." She hugged her once more and led her back inside.

Lea sat at the table, but she was no longer hungry. Her thoughts were on the murky future that lay ahead of her like a foggy bay.

Priscilla patted her hand a few times during the rest of the meal and motioned to a platter of food now and then.

She obliged only to stop drawing attention to herself.

Paul and the rest of the men spoke in excited tones as they planned for the next several months of journeys.

Lea let her attention be drawn as many times as she dared to Timothy only in hopes of memorizing his features before he disappeared down the Cayster River and out of her life for good.

The lamps under the columns of Arcadian Street were being lit when Lea was finally able to pull herself away from Priscilla. They had spent the hottest part of the day together and she had helped them at their booth in the market place afterward. When the streets became less crowded, Lea had gone down to the bay. It was a quiet place to pray and listen for the leading of Yahweh. Now that it was growing dark, it was time to face her fears.

The way to her home seemed far too short and she was standing at her own door before she could summon much courage. "Help me, Yahweh." She slipped off her sandals and entered.

Her father was sitting in one of the common rooms looking over a parchment.

"Abba."

He looked up at her.

"There is something I need to discuss with you."

He laid the scroll aside. "Shall we call your mother in?"

"No." Lea barely had the strength to face him alone. Both sets of parental eyes would be enough to keep her quiet. "I was hoping to speak to you in private first."

"Very well." He leaned back. "You may speak."

She took a few small steps across the room. "As you know, I've spent a great deal of time with Priscilla and the others." She dared a slight peek at him.

His face remained unchanged.

"Several months ago, I professed Jesus as Messiah and requested to be baptized by Paul. Since then, I have spent many days with Priscilla learning about the Way. I believe it has helped me grow in my knowledge of Yahweh and in my faith."

Lea glanced at her father for an argument.

"You're telling me you're a Way follower?"

She nodded. "I've heard and seen what faith in Jesus can do. I wanted the joy and peace that Priscilla and the others seem to have that I didn't."

He adjusted in his seat.

"Since believing in Jesus, the holy scrolls have come alive for me. The stories of Yahweh and all He has done make so much more sense. Everything fits together when you come to the conclusion that Jesus is Messiah."

"At least you have not neglected our traditions."

"I don't wish to cease. Jesus was a Jew too. He taught about fulfilling the law, not breaking it."

"There is much you don't understand."

"That is what I have come to speak to you about. Paul has been speaking at the school of Tyrannus after the mid-day meal and I wish to hear him. They will not be with us much longer and I want to take the opportunity to learn what I can."

"He is still teaching?"

"Every day in the school. He explains more about Jesus and reveals passages like I've never heard."

"To women as well?"

"To any who show up."

"Is that all you wish to speak with me about?"

She hesitated. There was far more she wanted to say. She wanted to beg him for his blessing to unite her with Timothy, but their traditions wouldn't have it. She chose another piece of honesty. "My prayer recently has been that you and the rest of our family would come to the Way. Though I know it seems scary and like you're turning your back on your people, but it's not. It's opened my eyes, my heart, my soul to a God I've worshiped my entire life. Following Jesus has washed my soul and made me feel brand new. When I came up out of that water, I was a new person. I only want the same for you."

He rubbed his beard in thought so long Lea lost count of how many times she shifted her weight in anticipation.

"I hope you understand the predicament you have placed me in. My daughter should be studying to become the best wife and mother she could be."

She nodded, but her stomach flipped.

"Though you have always been different from your sisters, you have remained respectful to your family." He folded his hands. "The followers of the Way have calmed since their arrival. I know I can't stop them from their meetings just like I can't stop the sea from turning.

"As long as things remain calm, I will allow you to attend their meetings so long as it doesn't interfere with your chores or synagogue meetings. With our household down to three, there is a lot less work to keep it running. I won't stand in the path of anyone learning more about Yahweh, especially my own daughter. Though I would caution you to test what they say against the traditions you have been taught."

"Thank you, Abba." She bowed deeply.

"Is it true they will be leaving soon?"

Lea swallowed the lump in her throat. "Yes."

"Good." He retrieved his parchment. "Then maybe things will return to normal here in Ephesus."

Lea hurried to her room and shut the door. She leaned against it and held her hands over her racing heart. She had done it. She had spoken honestly with her father and he had heard her. Though he was wrong about one thing. After coming to the Way, things would never be the same. Not for her at least.

Chapter Six

"So mightily grew the word of God and prevailed." -Acts 19:20

The evening meal was spread out before Lea, but her heart was not in eating. The silence of her parents hung heavy on her shoulders. She assumed Abba had told her mother of her decision. Neither had spoken to her all day.

Kelilah refilled Caleb's cup and set the clay pitcher a little too hard on the table.

Lea watched her father study her mother for a few moments before asking, "Is there something you'd like to say?"

"In fact, there is."

He waved her on.

She turned to Lea. "What has gotten into you?"

Lea looked to her father, but he didn't say anything.

"Your father tells me you have decided to follow the Way."

"Yes."

"He tells me you'd rather listen to that Paul of

yours than your own father."

Lea swallowed hard. "That's not what I said. I simply said I understand better." She felt a calm wash over her to settle her trembling body. "His words have pierced my soul and I have drawn closer to Yahweh because of his teaching."

"This can't be true," her mother protested. "It's that tent-making couple you've been spending time with."

"Yes, Ima. Priscilla and Aquila are Way followers as well."

"I knew it. I knew it was a bad idea to allow you to spend so much time with them."

"Abba?" She faced him.

He opened his mouth to speak, but a high-pitched scream came from outside.

The three rose from the table and stepped into the street.

A crowd gathered at a neighbor's house. In the center was a man surrounded by seven others.

"Those are Sceva's boys," Caleb explained. "What are they doing?"

"I command you in the name of Jesus whom Paul preaches to leave this man," the oldest brother ordered the man in the center.

"Jesus, I know," the man's voice was deep and unnatural. "And Paul I recognize, but who are you?" He leapt onto the oldest brother and tore at his clothes and skin.

Three of the other brothers attempted to remove him, but the man turned on them as well.

Caleb pushed Lea and Kelilah back toward their home.

"Rabbi Caleb." Gedaliah appeared through the crowd. "Come see what is happening at the Agora."

Kelilah went into the house, but Lea followed the two men down the street and toward the market place.

A massive fire lit up the empty space.

"You see, they are burning our city," Gedaliah explained to Caleb.

"Who?"

"Those Way followers," his tone held obvious disgust.

Rabbi Caleb pressed through the crowd. "What is the meaning of this?"

Lea shadowed him and saw Paul standing near the fire with Priscilla, Aquila, and Timothy. They watched as people stepped forward and tossed parchments into the flames.

Paul walked over to Caleb. "Greetings, Rabbi."

"You can keep your greeting and explain to me why you and your followers are endeavoring to burn down my city."

"I can assure you, Rabbi, that is not their intent."

"And just what is?"

"Those who have gathered here are bringing, of their own free will might I add, their parchments of spells."

"Spells?"

"They have come to confess Jesus as their Messiah and choosing to burn their practicing books as a display of faith."

"Totaling over fifty thousand pieces of silver," Gedaliah added.

Rabbi Caleb looked toward the man. "You're certain?"

"I've kept the sum myself."

"My fellow laborers and I were called here to witness their confessions," Paul clarified. "We will make sure the flames don't get out of control."

"I want this fire put out immediately."

"Of course, Rabbi. I'll see to it myself."

Caleb left without another word.

Lea looked at the group of people around the fire. She leaned over and whispered in Priscilla's ear. "They've all come to the Way?"

"Every last one of them."

"Praise Jesus."

The older woman looped her arm in Lea's. "Did you speak with your father?"

"I spoke with him the other night. He told my mother and she was giving her protest when a disturbance in the street drew us out. A man, I can only guess was controlled with an evil spirit, was attacking a group of brothers."

"Why?"

"They were trying to cast the evil spirit out."

"Did it work?"

"No. The spirit told them he recognized Jesus' name and Paul's, but didn't know who they were. Then he attacked all of them."

"Well, it *has* been an exciting night." She patted her hand. "Are you going to go back to speak with your family?"

She shrugged. "I shudder to think what Abba will have to say tonight after all of this."

Priscilla pulled her in close. "I will continue to pray for you. Yahweh will provide wisdom."

Timothy leaned around Aquila to look at them.

Lea smiled at him.

"I think our young friend has taken a shine to you," Priscilla's soft words danced in Lea's ears.

"I think I've found myself quite drawn to him as well." Lea watched the high flames lick up the parchments. "I still can't believe all of them came forward to follow the Way."

"Yahweh is moving in your city, Lea."

"I wish He would move in Abba's heart."

"We can pray He does. For if He can move in the hearts of so many, He can surely move in the heart of one of His own Rabbis."

"And on that day, I will certainly rejoice."

"As will we all."

Lea caught movement out of the corner of her eye and watched the crowd part. Even in the dim night, the flames brightened the red capes of the Roman guards.

"What is the meaning of this fire?" the commanding officer shouted.

"These have come to burn their own property," Paul responded.

"This needs to be extinguished at once or it will burn the entire city down."

A couple pushed themselves forward.

"These people have done nothing wrong," the husband explained.

"They have the right to burn their own belongings and are here as a testament to their God," the wife added.

The guard stepped up to the two. "I would suggest holding those Jewish tongues of yours unless you want me to have one of my men do it for you."

"You Roman dogs can't touch me!" the man shouted in his face.

Paul pressed himself between them. "Andronicus, take your wife and go home."

"We are here in the name of Jesus. These people have come to confess their sins and commit to the Way."

At the sound of that one word, hate lit in the soldier's face. "Arrest these for rioting and destruction of property."

The soldier closest to the woman grabbed her arm.

"Get your Roman hands off me!" she screamed and scratched him.

Another grabbed both Andronicus' arms and led him away.

"You can't do this." A man with them tried to remove the soldier's grip.

"Leave them alone!" Paul shouted. "They are Roman citizens."

"And these two as well." The commander pointed to Paul and the other man.

A third soldier took Paul into custody and led him away with the others.

"They can't do this, can they?" Lea asked Priscilla.

"Unfortunately, they can."

"Get this fire out now!" the commander shouted orders. "And clear out this place!"

Soldiers moved to fetch water while others pushed the crowd away.

Priscilla turned Lea around and the two huddled with the crowd until they could break away down the street toward the rented house.

Once the small group was safe inside, Aquila and Priscilla caught up in each other's arms.

"What are we going to do?" Priscilla wept into her husband's tunic.

"We are safe." He stroked her head. "Paul will be well. It's not the first time he's been imprisoned and it probably won't be the last."

Priscilla didn't appreciate her husband's attempt to lighten the mood and let him know by wailing louder.

Lea caught his eye over his wife's head and he shrugged.

"Did they hurt you?" Timothy stepped to Lea's side.

She tilted her head at him and then noticed she was rubbing her own arm. "Oh, no." She shook her head. "The guards didn't touch me. I got shoved into someone on the road and I guess I didn't realize how hard."

"Let me see it."

Lea looked to Aquila.

"It's alright," the older man assured her. "Timothy has spent a lot of time with Luke. He's picked up a few things."

Lea complied by holding out her arm.

Timothy raised her sleeve and gently worked his fingertips from her wrist to her shoulder and back down again.

His warm touch felt so inviting, Lea barely noticed the pain until he asked, "Does this hurt?"

"A little. It's not too bad."

Timothy worked up and down her arm. "I don't think it's broken."

"That's a relief."

"I do think we need to wrap it up for just a day or so to be safe." He waved to the table. "Sit down and I'll go find something."

"I'll fix you something to help with the discomfort." Priscilla was roused from her grief with a chance to put her hands to work.

"You're very kind, but I don't need all this attention. I'm sure it will be well tomorrow."

"Still, let's not take the risk." Timothy sat next to her on the bench and carefully wrapped her arm. When he finished, he slid her sleeve down over the wrap to cover it.

"Here." Priscilla handed her a cup.

The contents were warm and smelled appealing. Lea drank it down in two gulps.

Priscilla smiled at her when she retrieved the cup.

Lea felt the warmth radiate down her middle.

The group sat quietly each processing the events.

"Paul said something about the other people who were arrested with him," Lea wondered out loud.

"Two were relatives of his from Rome," she explained. "Andronicus and his wife, Junia. They came to the Way several years before Paul. The third was his former companion, John Mark. They told us…" Priscilla couldn't finish her thought.

"Our other companion, Barnabus, had been stoned to death," Aquila said.

"Poor Barnabus."

"Poor John Mark," Priscilla clarified. "He witnessed the whole thing." She dabbed her eyes. "Andronicus and Junia came to the area to teach. They brought John Mark to Paul to see what would become of the young man."

"A fine welcome," Aquila joked.

Tychicus came in from one of the back rooms. "Where's Paul?"

"He's been arrested," Priscilla explained. "Along with his cousins."

"They just arrived. What happened?"

"You know the temper on those two," Aquila added. "They spoke out against some Romans who were trying to stop a fire."

Tychicus rubbed his temples with his fingertips. "From the beginning, please."

"Some new Way followers were burning their spell scrolls in the Agora," Lea answered. "When the Romans came to investigate, Paul's cousins spoke out. They arrested them and when Paul tried to stop them, he was arrested too."

He sat down and put his head in his hands. "Not again."

"We'll visit him in the morning," Aquila said.

"Timothy and Tychicus."

Both men looked up.

"Will you please escort Lea to her home. With the events of tonight, I want to make sure she is safe."

The two men rose to accompany her.

"The last thing we need is to get on Rabbi Caleb's bad side."

"That is an easy thing to do," Lea agreed and set off toward home with her two bodyguards.

Chapter Seven

"Paul, a prisoner of Jesus Christ, and Timothy our brother, unto Philemon our dearly beloved, and fellowlabourer,"
-Philemon 1:1

Opening her shoulder bag, Lea carefully packed a stack of freshly baked bread. Though the familiar scents of a busy kitchen helped, the rented house felt empty. Paul had been in prison for days with no end in sight. The Romans were taking their time setting a hearing. Without him, the house was quieter and less joyous. Even Aquila's jokes lessened with the passing of days.

Priscilla and Aquila were at the market selling skins. She had arrived at the empty house, let herself in, and began preparing a care package for Paul. If nothing else, at least she could see to it that he ate properly while in chains. She left extras behind for the tent-making couple to come home to for their mid-day break.

The front door creaked open and Tychicus let himself in.

"Lea, I wasn't expecting you."

Another man followed him.

"I was making some food for Paul."

"That is very kind of you."

She looked to the other man who stared at the piles of food.

"This is Onesimus," Tychicus introduced his companion. "He's from Colossae."

Lea looked the man over. He was as rough as an ill-treated ox. Though massive in size, his eyes darted around as if frightened of some unseen threat.

"Why don't you sit, friend," Tychicus offered.

The man walked around the large table and chose to sit facing the door.

"Would you mind getting him some food? He hasn't had a good meal in a while."

"My pleasure." She prepared a bowl and broke off a large piece of bread.

The man watched her cautiously as she set the items in front of him.

"She won't hurt you," Tychicus assured him. "Go ahead and eat."

The man needed no further prompting to dig into the meal.

Tychicus followed Lea deeper into the kitchen.

"Is he ill?"

"Far from it," Tychicus explained. "He is a runaway slave."

"A what?"

He pushed his hands up and down in front of her, signaling for her to lower her voice. "He ran to Ephesus hoping to get away from his master. He happened to go into Tyrannus' school and hear Paul speak last week. We think he was looking for food left behind. Instead, he found the bread of life."

"You mean he became a Way follower?"

"That very day."

"He claimed sanctuary with Paul while they tried to figure out a plan." He peered into the other room. "I went searching for him when Paul was arrested."

"What's going to happen to him?"

"I'm going to see Paul now. We are planning to write a letter to his master asking for grace. Paul has challenged me with delivering him back to Colossae."

"You're leaving?"

He turned back to her. "For a short season. Paul is writing letters as we speak. It'll be my duty to deliver them along with our friend in there."

"Could I accompany you?"

He opened his mouth then closed it.

"I mean to the prison."

He shook his head. "I don't think that's a good idea."

"Please? I want to see Paul."

"Alright. You can accompany me and I'll leave Onesimus here for now." He walked back to the table. "Lea and I are going to see Paul," he told the slave. "Stay here and lock the door. Don't let anyone in until I return for you."

The man nodded.

Lea prepared another bowl for him and broke a larger piece of bread. She smiled as she placed it on the table.

He kept his eyes on the food.

"You'll need your strength." She grabbed her bag and placed a cloth over the remaining piles.

The square tower stood tall and proud as they arrived at the prison.

"We are here to see Paul," Tychicus said to the guard.

He gave Lea a long glance before sending them back to the cells.

Lea stayed close to Tychicus as they walked the narrow hallway. She didn't dare look into the other cells as they passed. The smell of rotting flesh and unclean chamber pots had her covering her face with her headwrap. The heat pressed in around her as she kept on her friend's heels.

Paul's cell was not hard to find as Timothy was set up just outside of it with a small table.

Tychicus greeted him.

"I have something for Paul." Lea lifted the strap over her head and handed the bag to

Timothy.

He peered inside and smiled. "I'm sure he'll appreciate the offering." He stepped closer to the cell and lifted the bag through the opening. "Lea brought you some provisions."

"Young one," a hoarse voice called from behind the door.

Lea lifted herself onto her toes to see into the room through the small barred opening that was ajar. Paul stood with chains hanging from his hands and binding his feet together. His tunic was dirty and his face was covered in dust, but his smile was bright.

"Thank you for the gift."

"I hate seeing you in chains."

"I will never be ashamed of what they do to me while I spread the message of Jesus." He coughed.

She backed up and pulled Tychicus to the side. "Is he ill?"

He shook his head. "He's been dictating letters. It's left his throat sore."

She watched Timothy set to work scribing again.

"Why isn't he writing them?"

"Paul's eyesight has been getting worse ever since a nasty eye infection in Galatia. He had just come from being stoned and I think he wasn't strong enough to keep going, but he did. The followers there were so gracious to him though.

They offered to pluck out their own eyes and give them to him."

"They must love him a great deal." She looked to the one who sat scribing the words of his mentor who was from the area of Galatia himself.

"Luke has been treating him, but it continues to grow worse."

"I see him reading scrolls all the time."

"He's not completely blind. Though he has simply memorized most of those writings." He leaned against the wall. "Luke usually scribes for him, but he is still in Philippi so he's asked Timothy to do it."

"How long do you think he's going to be here?"

"Hard to tell. He has hope though."

"Ready for the next letter," Timothy said.

"I'd like to write this one myself." Paul stretched his fingers through the opening.

"Are you sure?"

"It will have more weight if it comes from my own hand."

Timothy slipped a piece of parchment and a quill through the opening.

"Who's he writing to?" Tychicus asked.

"Philemon," Timothy explained.

"I'm ready to take those letters as soon as he's done."

"Is Onesimus secure?"

"As secure as I could make him."

"And your passage?"

"Ready to leave when we are."

"I hope Paul's right about this last letter. I pray Philemon has mercy on Onesimus."

Lea prayed for the man sitting in the rented house. She couldn't imagine the things he had endured. The risk of being sold into slavery fell over her like a weight. She finally realized how foolish she had acted and why her family had warned her to be cautious. Tears filled her eyes. The idea of sharing the fate of the man she had just met hurt her heart.

Pour out grace from his master, she prayed. *Only you, Yahweh, could see to it that he receives mercy instead of judgment.*

"Finished." Paul pushed the parchment to Timothy.

Lea dried her eyes.

Timothy passed the stack of scrolls to Tychicus. "This is all of them."

"May Yahweh smile on your journey, dear brother," Paul spoke from his cell.

"I'll return when my mission is complete," he promised and left.

"Is there anything else I can do for you?" Lea lifted herself to speak through the opening.

"Pray, young one. Yahweh will hear."

She did just that on her way back to the rented

house.

When she arrived, Onesimus was gone along with Tychicus. It was too early for the mid-day break and the house didn't need any more cleaning. She sat at the large, empty table praying for all her friends.

A knock startled her. On the other side of the door stood her sister, Zahara.

"Come in." She waved and shut the door behind her.

"I came to the house for a visit. Ima told me where I could probably find you."

"Is everything well with the boys?"

"Oh yes, they are well." Zahara walked around the room as if in search of something.

"To what do I owe this visit?"

"Ima says you've been spending a lot of time with these people."

"They have become like family."

Her sister stopped. "And what of your real family?"

"I didn't mean it like that," she tried to explain. "It's like my family has grown. Like every time I got a new brother-in-law."

"I see."

Zahara lapped the room again.

"Is there something you're looking for?"

"I had an interesting talk with Isaiah this morning."

"Did he ask for one of my stories?"

"Not exactly." She sat at the table. "He told me a story."

Lea joined her. "Oh?"

"He said the day he was sick you came to visit him."

"I remember."

"He also said he had another visitor."

Lea lifted her eyebrow.

"He said he could hear you and Noam speaking, but your voices were muffled. You left for a while, but when you came back you put something on his head."

Lea folded her fingers. Her heart started pounding.

"He said that when you did, another man was in the room. Someone he didn't know, but was very kind to him." Tears streamed down her face. "He said the man asked him whether he wanted to go with him or stay with us."

"What did he tell him?"

"He told the man he didn't want to make me sad by leaving, so he wanted to stay." She looked up into Lea's eyes. "Who did you bring to see my son?"

"I didn't bring anyone."

"Then who was in the room?"

Lea thought. "Did Isaiah tell you anything else?"

"He said the man was very shiny and it was hard to see his face."

The hairs on Lea's arm rose. "I think I know who stood before your son."

"Tell me."

"I did leave as he said. I came here to retrieve Paul so he could pray over Isaiah. He's done it for so many others. But Paul was in a meeting and couldn't leave. He sent me back with a cloth."

"A cloth?"

"I know it sounds mad, but it's true. He instructed me that if I would place the cloth on Isaiah, then he would be made whole in Je—" She held her tongue.

"What?"

Lea looked down. "In Jesus' name." She looked back up at her sister. "I tried to tell Isaiah, but Noam stopped me. He told me he didn't want the boys to hear about Jesus."

"You're saying you believe Jesus healed Isaiah?"

She nodded. "I believe it was He who also stood in the room though only Isaiah saw Him. Paul told me that it wasn't the cloth that held the power, but the name of Jesus and my faith in Him that provided the healing."

"Your faith in Jesus?"

"I became a Way follower some time ago."

Zahara rubbed her face. "A Way follower?

Does Abba know?"

"He does. He wasn't happy about it, but I've done everything he has asked, including attending all synagogue meetings. Since Paul's arrest, I've been avoiding Abba. Before that, I'd been meeting once a day to hear Paul teach. Sister, the scrolls have come alive to me under his teachings. To hear all that Jesus did and said. He is Messiah."

"He's dead. They crucified him."

"They did, but on the third day He walked out of that grave. He was seen of hundreds of witnesses."

"So, where is He now?"

"After several days with His disciples, they say He ascended back into the heavens to prepare to come again as a judge."

"He's coming back?"

"Yes!" She wanted to sing. "But we must be ready. It's like…" she thought for a few moments. "Like how we have to be ready when a bridegroom comes for his wife. We don't know when he's going to come so we have to stay ready. Jesus didn't tell us when He's coming, but made a promise to return for us."

"So how do we get ready?"

"Do you remember when you were preparing for Noam's arrival?"

"Yes." A slight smile crept up her lips. "It seems like so long ago."

"And do you remember when we heard the shofar that I didn't have a nice dress to wear?"

Zahara rubbed her chin. "Nava gave you one of hers."

"Exactly! I wasn't ready to go to the wedding feast dressed the way I was. Nava gave me one of her festive dresses so I could be ready. It's like that with Jesus."

"He gives us a new dress?"

"Sort of. We are not dressed for His wedding feast, that's going to Heaven, and all our garments are like filthy rags. He gives us a new garment so that we can be ready when He comes to get His bride."

"And how do you get this new garment?"

"You have to believe that Jesus is Messiah and ask for His forgiveness."

"What about all our ancestors? Do you not believe they are with Yahweh?"

Lea bit her lip. "Paul explained that to me once. He said they had to have faith just like we do. They had to have faith in the Messiah who was coming and we have to have faith in the Messiah that came and is coming again."

"Why can't we just trust Yahweh?"

"Yahweh is holy and can't be reached by us sinful people. We need a mediator, like the priests, to get to Yahweh. That's Jesus."

"But we have priests and sacrifices in the

temple."

"Those were always meant to be a representation of Messiah. Jesus came as our Passover Lamb to shed His blood once for all our sins. He is our High Priest who takes our requests to the throne of Yahweh. He also clothes us in His righteousness so that we can stand in the presence of Yahweh."

"You believe this?"

"All of it. Hearing the message of the Way pricked my heart. I confessed my belief and Paul baptized me. From that day on, I've been so different. I'm not afraid anymore of what life has for me. My joy is endless. The others have become like brothers and sisters to me. Paul said it's because we all have the Holy Spirit residing in us that binds us together."

"The Holy what?"

"The Holy Spirit of God. When Jesus left, He gave a gift to his disciples. Like how a bridegroom leaves behind a token to remind his bride of the promise of his return. He said another would come that would indwell believers and be our comforter, our guide, our help, and so much more. The Holy Spirit."

"Like Yahweh's Spirit resting on Samson?"

"Yes. Except He doesn't have seasons of rest. He actually permanently dwells in us after we come to faith in Jesus."

Zahara sat in silence for a long time.

Lea counted her own heartbeats waiting for her sister to speak.

"How do you know whether Jesus will accept you?"

"That's the easy part," she said softly. "He told us He would freely accept anyone who comes to Him."

"Anyone?"

"Anyone."

"Even a lowly housewife with two boys?"

Lea's heart thudded. "Sister, are you saying what I think you're saying?"

She nodded. "I want what you have, Lea. I've seen how different you are since coming to the Way. Your face shines and you have so much peace. I don't have that. I saw the joy in Isaiah's face when he spoke of the man in his room. If it's this Jesus that you spoke about, I want to know Him too."

Voices came from the other side of the door before it opened.

Lea rose.

Priscilla and Aquila entered.

"She wants to confess Jesus," Lea rushed on without explanation.

Priscilla looked behind her to the woman who still sat at the table. "Who is she?"

"My sister. She wants to be a Way follower."

"Praise Yahweh!" Aquila shouted. "I'll baptize you myself."

"Right now?"

"If there is one thing I've learned in all my time on this earth, it's to not put things off."

"First things first, Husband," Priscilla interjected. "I believe introductions are in order."

"This is my oldest sister, Zahara," Lea explained. "Zahara, these are my friends Priscilla and Aquila."

Zahara rose and stood next to her sister. "It's nice to finally meet you."

"Now, Zahara." Priscilla folded her hands. "Do you believe Jesus is Messiah?"

She looked to her sister and then back to her. "Yes."

"Do you believe He was crucified, buried, and on the third day rose again?"

"I do."

"Do you confess your sins and believe He has atoned for them with His blood?"

"Yes."

"Then I welcome you, sister, into our family." She hugged her.

"Now we can baptize you." Aquila held the door open for the women.

Lea watched her sister go down into the water a curious woman and come up a sister the second time around. As she wrapped her in a dry cloth,

Lea noticed the beaming smile that lit up her sister's face.

"Is this that joy we were talking about?" Zahara asked.

"Yes. No matter what happens, that joy will always remain. The Holy Spirit will give you peace beyond anything you've ever experienced. Welcome to the family."

Chapter Eight

"A bishop then must be blameless, the husband of one wife, vigilant, sober, of good behaviour, given to hospitality, apt to teach;"
-1 Timothy 3:2

Lea finished her chores early and made her way to Pricilla's booth in the Agora.

"It's busy today," she remarked, pressing herself close to their stall.

"That it is." Pricilla held up a skin for the customer she was helping.

"Would you like me to get a head start on the mid-day meal? I'm all done at home."

"Would you?" She wiped her brow. "I was afraid I'd have to leave Aquila alone to handle this crowd."

"It would be a pleasure to help."

"Thank you. You know where everything is, go ahead and let yourself in."

Weaving her way through the pressing flow of people, Lea deposited her sandals at Priscilla's door and walked inside.

"Oh," she said. "Forgive me."

Timothy sat by himself. The large table in front of him was covered with scrolls and parchments.

"I would have knocked, but I didn't realize anyone would be here."

"Come in." He waved. "I'm just studying. Are you looking for Priscilla?"

"No." She blushed. "I've already been to see her. The market place is busy so they are trying to take advantage of the crowd."

"Paul no doubt praying for financial blessings for the upcoming travels." He chuckled to himself.

The reminder caught Lea's breath.

"Are you well?" He rose.

"No." She held up her hands. "I mean, yes, I'm well."

"You're sure?"

"Yes." She attempted a smile.

He hesitated, but returned to his seat. "So, what brings you by so early?"

"I finished my chores and was going to spend some time by the bay, but when I saw how busy Pricilla was, I offered to come prepare for the midday meal."

"How thoughtful of you." His eyes brightened with his broad smile. "By all means, go ahead. Pricilla drew some fresh water before they left."

She bowed and scrubbed her hands. After selecting the vegetables and spices, she set to work peeling and cutting. One thing Priscilla's kitchen was never low on was meat. Spending her days at a tanner's table guaranteed the freshest of meat. The surplus was often traded with local fishermen for fresh fish. Lea thought her mother's kitchen was pleasantly stocked, but even her wealthy family would envy such a bounty.

Timothy looked up from his studies and over his shoulder at her. "Priscilla mentioned you enjoy spending time at the bay."

"Oh yes." Her cheeks grew warm.

"What draws you there?"

"The people mostly. I like watching new faces come in and out. I play a…" She paused. Timothy was so easy to talk to she almost forgot how trivial her thoughts might sound out loud, especially to a man who's traveled the world.

"You play a what?"

"It's silly."

"Come now."

She looked down at the onion in her hand. "I play a game to see if I can guess where people are coming from who visit our city."

"That doesn't sound silly at all. How often are you right?"

"Fairly often." She set the onion on the counter and started chopping.

"Is that all that draws you there?"

She wavered. "No." Her thoughts drifted like

the ships down the river. "The idea of what could be waiting out there also calls me."

"You've got an adventurous spirit."

She pressed the knife down hard and shook her head. "Doesn't matter."

"I'm sorry?"

"Forget it."

"No, please." He turned so that his entire body faced her. "Please tell me."

She set down the knife and took a deep breath. "It doesn't matter that I feel led away. The longing in my heart that has been there since I can remember has only grown since Paul came to Ephesus.

"None of it matters because I'm the daughter of Rabbi Caleb. My place is to do my duty until I'm packaged off to the highest bidder." Tears formed. "Some days I'd rather any other fate than tied to a man's side like a ship tied to a dock." She spun around to face Timothy.

His kind eyes held her gaze. He wasn't angry at her fury. He simply sat listening to her honest outpouring.

She blinked away the dampness from her eyes. "Forgive me. I didn't mean to…"

"It's alright. We should all be heard."

"Not according to my father."

"Though I've only been here a short time, I don't think your father is as harsh as you imagine.

He might simply be trying his best to protect you."

"I know." She sighed.

He was quiet for a few moments. "Do you know what your name means?"

"In Hebrew, it means 'tired.' Though I don't know if they chose the name because my mother was tired from delivery or my father was tired of having girls."

Timothy laughed and patted his leg.

Lea's heart lightened at the sound.

"Do you want to know what it means in Greek?"

She tilted her head.

"It means 'bringer of good news.' "

"Now you're the one playing games."

"I'm being honest."

She thought on his words and it made her smile.

"Yahweh has a plan for you, Lea. Your name might be a sign of what lies ahead on your path."

"I don't understand."

"Why would He name you 'bringer of good news' and put a call in your heart to go if He was going to bind you?"

"If only I could hope."

"Hope is a very powerful thing. Never forget that."

She nodded and turned back to the food.

"What are you studying?"

"Paul left me a few of his scrolls regarding the prophet Isaiah."

"Those are some of my favorites."

"Mine too. I'm studying the part about the suffering servant Paul spoke about several months ago."

"I enjoyed that very much. When he explained how Jesus suffered exactly like the way Isaiah described, it really made the words come alive."

"Jesus is all over our scrolls." He waved over the stack in front of him.

"Paul is a great teacher. You're lucky to be able to study under him."

"I'm blessed."

"You know I have a young nephew named after the prophet."

"The one who was sick?"

She nodded. "He's much better now. Like a new child."

"I'm happy Jesus healed him."

"So am I. I don't know what I would have done with myself if that little boy had not been spared. I've known him from his birth. He is like my very own."

"Would you like your own?"

She glanced at him over her shoulder. "Someday. For now, I get to spoil my two nephews and hope that my other sisters will soon give me more."

He chuckled. "How many sisters do you have?"

"I'm the youngest of four."

"Bless your father."

"Sometimes, I don't think he sees us as blessings."

"That's not true. I'm sure your father counts his four blessings every morning."

"Perhaps. I know he wished for sons, but he is a pretty proud grandfather none the less."

"I'd like to be a Saba one day too."

"Do you have any siblings?"

"I'm afraid not. It's just me."

"How sad."

"Yes and no. I would have liked siblings to share my childhood days, but being the sole focus of my Safta Lois and Ima did much to keep my focus on Yahweh."

"It has served you well."

"Plus, there was never a short supply of children in my town to play with," he joked.

"I'd like to visit Lystra."

"Would you?"

"I'd like to visit lots of places. It's always been a dream of mine to travel."

"Then why don't you?"

She returned her attention to cooking. "My place is here until I am released from my father's house. Such wishes can only remain dreams. A Rabbi's daughter will be a great prize for some man."

"Hope can turn dreams into reality."

She dumped a handful of vegetables into a pot and then turned to look at him.

"And so can Yahweh." He returned his attention to his studies.

As the meal came together, her thoughts stayed on the things Timothy said. She did want to hope, but life had thrown a few too many jars of water on that fire.

When the sun found its highest point, the tentmakers came home to feast.

"This looks wonderful." Priscilla spread her arms over the table.

Lea set out the last platter. "Happy to help."

Aquila sniffed. "Sure smells inviting."

"Please, sit."

He made himself comfortable with Timothy, who had cleared his materials in time for their return.

"I had forgotten about his plans to study today," Priscilla whispered near Lea as she filled the cups with water.

"It turned out well." She smiled. "We got a chance to talk."

"A pleasant time, I hope."

"Very."

"Good. I know Paul and Aquila have both taken time to speak with him."

"Talking will not fix everything."

"Patience." She sat beside her husband.

Lea sat and listen to Aquila pray for Paul and those sitting in chains.

"How did the rest of the morning go?" she asked as they ate.

"Very profitable," Aquila answered. "We stopped to visit Paul on our way home. He is happy with the progress of our funds."

Lea's stomach flopped and she swallowed down the lump in her throat.

Priscilla patted her arm. "Trust."

She nodded and reached for a platter.

"This stew is delicious." Aquila lifted a piece of soaked bread to her.

"Thank you. It's nothing special."

"It's wonderful," Timothy added.

She felt her cheeks flush. "Who will speak in Paul's place today?" Lea attempted to distract herself from Timothy's gaze.

"Timothy," Aquila answered.

"Oh? What will you be teaching on?"

"Jesus' resurrection."

"Is it true the Jews crucified Him because He claimed to be a god?"

"He wasn't the only one who claimed to be deity," Aquila remarked. "Herod Antipas did as well. But Jesus was the only one of them who walked out of the grave."

Timothy choked on his stew laughing.

Lea joined in.

"Jesus didn't just claim to be a god," Timothy explained after composing himself. "But equal with Yahweh Himself."

"And that's why they called for His blood?" she asked.

"You have a lot of questions." He smiled at her.

"Ones I'm hoping to learn the answers to today."

"Then let's fill our bellies," Aquila said. "So we can fill our minds."

The group ate until they were full and made their way across town to the large school. For the next several hours, Lea listened to Timothy expound on the ancient scrolls of her people and explained the teachings of Jesus.

When the workday began again, Lea joined the tentmakers at their booth to lend an extra set of hands. It felt good to be productive. Though every coin she added to their money pouch made her heart sick with sorrow. Each one would mean one less day they would spend with her.

As Priscilla and Aquila packed up their goods, Lea excused herself to spend some time at the bay.

The cool sea breeze did much to calm her

anxious heart. She sat on the stone wall with her feet over the side watching the last ships of the day depart. While they sailed away, she lifted her burdens to Yahweh.

"I can see what you mean," a familiar voice said behind her.

She didn't have to turn around to know it was Timothy who was next to her.

"It's so peaceful out here." He sat on the wall leaving a respectful amount of room between them. "I've never stopped and watched like this before."

She closed her eyes and let the wind play with her hair. "It's one of my favorite places."

"Seen any good people today?"

"Actually, I wasn't really watching people today."

"No?"

"I was using the peace to pray."

"An excellent thing to do."

She opened her eyes and looked at him. "Thank you for your words earlier. They have helped me renew my hope."

He smiled and turned toward the river.

They sat in silence watching the water until the sun set and the street lamps were lit.

"I suppose I should get home." She stood. "My parents will be expecting me."

Timothy rose. "May I walk you home?"

She froze. "Home?"

"To your house." He chuckled supposing she was joking.

"My house?" She shook away the fear that crawled inside her. "S-s-sure."

He bowed and waved his arm toward the road. "Shall we?"

She walked stiffly up Arcadian Street practically holding her breath. Dread of the moment simply being a dream crossed her mind more than once on the path.

"This is my father's house." She pointed to the large villa.

Lea slipped off her sandals and put her hand on the wooden door.

Timothy stood behind her.

"Is everything alright?" She glanced over her shoulder.

"I'd like to meet your parents. If you'd allow me."

Her eyes grew large. "You want to meet my family?"

"Very much. I mean I've spoken with your father a few times, but we've not been officially introduced."

"I see."

"Well?"

She looked to the door. "Oh. Yes, of course." She leaned on the door and welcomed him in.

"Abba?" she called.

Rabbi Caleb entered the main area.

Lea watched his face rise in alarm, but he brought it under control quickly.

"Daughter, who is our guest?"

"This is one of Paul's traveling companions, Timothy."

He bowed to the older man. "It's a pleasure to finally meet you, Rabbi."

"I've heard much about you, young man."

Lea caught his emphasis on the word *young*.

"Caleb, who's—Oh Lea it's you." Kelilah entered from the kitchen.

"This is Timothy," Caleb explained. "One of Paul's followers."

Lea exchanged a pleading glance with her mother.

"Well, come in," Kelilah offered. "You two must be starving. I was just getting some food on the table."

Lea hurried past her father. "Thank you, Ima," she whispered as they made their way to the table.

"If there is one thing I'm used to as a Rabbi's wife, it's visitors."

Caleb spoke a blessing and welcomed them to eat.

Lea helped her mother serve.

"So, I hear you and your companions won't be with us much longer," Caleb said.

Timothy glanced quickly at Lea before answering, "That's true. We are raising funds now for our next journey."

"And where will that be?" He took a bite.

"The plan is to visit Corinth and some of the other churches in Macedonia. Paul wishes to collect funds for the poor in Jerusalem. We will stop there before journeying on to Jerusalem and then finally on to Rome. Maybe even Spain. We will see how far Yahweh allows us."

"Rome, you say?"

"Yes. Emperor Nero is allowing Jews back into Rome. Paul feels led to go, so we go."

"I see."

"Where are you from?" Kelilah asked.

"Lystra. My father, mother, and grandmother still reside there."

"You must not get to see them much."

"Not as often as I'd like. But I'm hoping to fit in a visit with them on our travels."

"I'm sure they are looking forward to seeing you." She poured some more water for Caleb. "How has your time in Ephesus been?"

"I'm enjoying my time here very much." He glanced to Lea again.

"To what do we owe this visit?" Caleb's voice deepened.

Lea furrowed her brow and wanted to speak up, but thought better of it. She stared at the enormous fish on the platter in front of her. She would rather trade places with it than remain silent during Timothy's interrogation.

"Surely there is a reason you've come to us now after you've lived in our city for nearly a year."

Lea looked to her mother with beseeching eyes.

"Actually, there is something that has brought me here this evening."

She tilted her head at him.

"I've come to ask for a betrothal agreement for your daughter."

Caleb stood in a quick motion. "No."

"Abba!" Lea protested, but swiftly covered her mouth.

"I will not have my daughter be married to a Greek." He waved his hands in front of himself. "Absolutely not."

"I'm only half Greek by birth, Rabbi. From my youth, I have stayed true to the practice of our traditions."

"But you choose the Way over our traditions." Caleb crossed his arms over his chest.

"It is true that I am a follower of Jesus, but I don't consider that a replacement for my Jewish faith. I believe Jesus is the fulfillment of everything Yahweh promised to the Jews."

"The lies your people tell." He huffed.

"Do you have another betrothal for your daughter?"

Caleb's face turned bright red. "No," he ground out.

"I have adequate payment and care a great deal for Lea."

"You barely know her."

"The little time I have spent with your daughter, I've seen the wonderful woman she has become. No doubt a testament to you and your wife."

"I don't bend to flattery, young man."

"That is not my intent. I simply mean that I have seen all I need to see. I believe Lea would make a wonderful wife and partner. If she'd be a willing one."

Lea watched the exchange as if she were a spectator in the theater. She wanted to scream her agreement from the top of the Temple of Diana.

Caleb looked to his wife first and then to his daughter before returning his attention back to Timothy. He gradually sat. "What life could you give my daughter when you blow about from place to place like the wind?"

"I've thought about that a lot. It's honestly one of the reasons why it's taken me so long to make this request. I don't have a good enough answer."

"And you expect me to hand over my last daughter to you?"

"I'm asking you to consider it."

Caleb patted down his long beard. "I will consider it."

A tiny spark inside Lea caught fire. Timothy was right, hope was powerful.

Chapter Nine

"And the LORD God said, It is not good that the man should be alone; I will make him an help meet for him." -Genesis 2:18

A knock on the front door drew Lea from her bedroom to answer it.

Timothy stood on the steps with his mentor.

"Paul?" Lea clutched the older man. "What happened? Another rescue by an angel?"

Paul chuckled. "Nothing quite so miraculous."

"He has been released," Timothy explained.

"I'm so happy to see you free."

"And I'm happy to see you, young one." He held her face in his hands and kissed the top of her head.

"What finally made them change their minds?" Lea wondered.

"Priscilla and Aquila," Timothy said.

"It seems I owe my neck to the two of them." Paul rubbed his throat. "They almost lost theirs in rescuing mine."

"Are they alright?"

"Yes, yes." Paul patted her shoulder. "All is

well now."

"And what of Andronicus and Junia?"

"They've been freed as well," Timothy answered.

She clasped her hands. "Praise Yahweh. And John Mark? What is to become of him?"

"He'll stay close by," Paul said. "He feels lead to serve here in Ephesus with us. I think it will be good for him to remain near us."

"I'm so glad you stopped by to deliver this news."

Timothy and Paul exchanged a glance.

"Is there more?"

"I'm actually here to see your father," Paul clarified. "Is the Rabbi here?"

"Of course. Please come in."

The two followed her into the main room where Rabbi Caleb sat looking over his parchments. He stood when they came close.

Paul bowed. "Greetings, Rabbi Caleb. I beseech you for a meeting."

He lifted an eyebrow at Timothy who stood behind Paul. "Lea, is your mother home?"

"She just left for the Agora."

"Prepare a snack then."

"Yes, Abba." She rushed to the kitchen and set out a platter of dried figs and goat cheese along with fresh water cups.

Caleb sat on one side of the table while Paul

and Timothy sat on the other.

Lea busied her hands with meal preparations her mother had left so she would have an excuse to stay in the kitchen.

"It is good to hear of your release." Caleb chewed on a fig. "To what do I owe this visit?"

"I've come to negotiate a betrothal."

Caleb choked on the bite in his mouth. He pounded his chest and took a long sip of water. "Pardon me?"

Paul waited while Caleb composed himself. "I've come as father to Timothy to negotiate his betrothal to your daughter, Lea."

"You've been out of prison mere hours and you come to my home to discuss marriage? Doesn't the boy already have a father?"

"He does. Though a good man, Hector is not only far from here, but also not a Jewish man that he may make these negotiations." Paul gripped Timothy's shoulder. "This boy has been like a son to me from the day we met. I have been his spiritual father and, as a legal Jewish male, I come to make these negotiations."

Lea watched her father's face darken to crimson and then cool before he spoke.

"Your *son* is also not a legal Jewish man."

"I can assure you he is. I circumcised him with my own hands and have witnessed his careful study and adherence to our traditions."

Caleb straightened his beard.

"We can pay whatever you ask as bride price and are here to discuss the details of their betrothal."

"I have not yet agreed to this offer."

Paul folded his hands on the table. "I understand Timothy came to you a few days ago."

"He did."

"And you told him you'd consider his offer."

"I did."

"Are there any other offers you are considering?"

"No."

Lea's heart dropped like a stone. Her worst fears were finally spoken. Her father had not been seeking a husband for her.

"I hoped a father figure would help move along these negotiations." Paul locked the Rabbi in a penetrating stare. "I'm also here to remind you that there is something you probably haven't considered."

"Oh?" Caleb's right eyebrow rose and fell quickly.

"Both of these young people are old enough to elope on their own without your permission."

Lea froze. She hadn't considered that either. It was true. She'd known others who took that path when they differed with their parents. It never seemed like a viable option for her. No man had ever held her heart until Timothy came into her life. She watched her father. He didn't move for several heartbeats.

"Rabbi Caleb," Timothy spoke softly as if trying to lure a frightened animal. "Paul and I have had many conversations over this matter. I shouldn't have come to you alone, but I knew my father would not have been a suitable negotiator. I understand that my actions may have caused unintentional disrespect. For that, I sincerely apologize.

"Paul has taken on the role of my father long before today. Upon his suggestion of a private marriage, I adamantly refused. Not only out of respect for you, but also your daughter. I'm sure she, as well as I, would rather have your blessing in this union instead of your contempt. So, I have asked Paul to act as my father in this arrangement."

Caleb nodded sharply.

Paul reached to his belt and untied his money pouch. "We are prepared today to pay Lea's bride price and write up the legal documents necessary."

Lea recognized the money pouch. It was the same one they deposited coins in from the sale of skins and tents.

"No."

"Pardon me?" Caleb turned to face his daughter.

Lasting Legacy

"I can't let them do this." She picked up Paul's pouch and handed it back to him.

"What are you saying?" her father asked.

"I know where the money is coming from for my bride price. Those coins are marked for Paul's travels. Those funds should be going to further the Way. It wouldn't be right." She pushed the bag closer to Paul. "I can't."

Timothy stood and came near her. He placed his palms on her cheeks.

Tears formed in her eyes and flowed down over his fingers. "I can't ask you to do this."

"You didn't ask," he reassured her. "I want to do this and Paul has graciously helped provide the path."

"But the funds—"

"Can be replaced." He used his thumbs to wipe away her tears. "You can't."

"But it will take time to replace all that money."

"It seems time is what we have, young one," Paul's voice was deep and calming. "If Timothy must be here to fulfill his betrothal year anyway, we shall use the time to replenish the funds and help prepare you two as well."

"That would mean another year here instead of doing the work Yahweh has called you to."

"And one year closer to you becoming my wife." Timothy smiled. "Yahweh has plenty of work for me here. I believe this is the path He has for me. The question is, do you believe it as well?"

"Lea?" Caleb rubbed his bearded chin.

She blinked back tears. "Yes, Abba?"

"Do you agree to this arrangement?"

She looked into Timothy's deep eyes. "I do."

"Well it seems we have two willing people and a legal negotiator. Though I have my doubts about you, young man. You may have the betrothal year to prove me wrong."

Lea's heart leapt for joy.

Timothy smiled for the first time since they walked through the door.

Caleb and Paul spoke in legal tones as Lea returned to her work.

Kelilah came home from the market as the document was being written. "You've agreed on a betrothal?"

"We have." Caleb showed her the money pouch.

"Then we must start preparing you, Lea."

"May I ask Priscilla to join us?" Les asked.

Kelilah looked at her husband.

"We will need witnesses for the betrothal ceremony. Call whom you wish."

After collecting Priscilla from her home, the three women made their way to the woman's bathhouse.

"My joy overflows for you." Priscilla squeezed

Lea's hand.

Kelilah and Priscilla brushed out Lea's hair.

"Is Timothy a good man?" her mother asked.

Priscilla patted her hand. "One of the best I know."

Lea carefully undressed and wrapped herself in a clean cloth.

"Ready?" Priscilla asked.

She nodded.

Lea entered the bath with the attendant. She stepped on the first stone step and handed over her wrap. The next few steps sent a shiver up her body as her bare feet tread on the cold stone. When her toes touched the warm spring water, she wanted to dive in, but continued her slow descent.

As the water rose to her chin, she paused. She peeked up at the attendant standing by. "Blessed are You, O Lord, our God, King of the universe, who has sanctified us with Your commandments and commanded us concerning the immersion."

As she had done after every one of her unclean times of the month, Lea immersed herself entirely in the water. When she broke the surface of the water again, the attendant turned her back to allow Lea a few moments of privacy.

The water reminded her of her baptism and a fresh wave of peace came over her. "Yahweh, thank You for the path You have set me on. Bless my union with Timothy. Help me be a good wife for him. Give my father's heart validation of this marriage."

She made her way to the steps and ascended to the attendant who had the dry cloth open and waiting for her.

The woman gently wrapped her up and whispered, "May Yahweh bless you."

She smiled warmly. "Thank you."

When she was dressed and ready, the two women led Lea back home where Caleb stood outside with the necessary preparations.

Timothy stood beside him with freshly damp hair. He had bathed across town in the men's bathhouse.

Aquila and Tychicus stood on Caleb's left as official witnesses. Priscilla and Kelilah walked Lea to Timothy's right side and then stepped away.

Rabbi Caleb placed a fabric over the two young people as a canopy.

Lea could feel the warmth of Timothy's body next to hers under the material. It felt inviting against her shivering skin.

Caleb retrieved a cup filled with wine from the front steps and blessed it, "Blessed are You, Adonai our God, Sovereign of all, Creator of the fruit of the vine.

"Blessed are You, Adonai our God, King of the universe, who has sanctified us with Your commandments and given us commandments concerning forbidden connections, and has forbidden unto us those who are merely betrothed, and permitted unto us those lawfully married to us through canopy and betrothal. Blessed are You, O Lord, who sanctifies Your people Israel."

He allowed Timothy a sip and then Lea before returning the cup to the step.

Timothy reached into his pouch and produced a simple ring.

Lea held out her right hand.

He slipped the symbol on her index finger and held it there. "With this ring, you are consecrated to me according to the law of Moses and Israel."

Rabbi Caleb carefully removed the canopy. "You are now legally bound to each other and only a bill of divorce may separate you."

Timothy turned to face Lea. "That won't happen," he whispered.

Priscilla and Kelilah took turns hugging and kissing on Lea. Both wiping away tears in between.

The men patted Timothy on the back and offered their congratulations.

Caleb stood at the bottom of the steps fingering the material in his hands.

Lea pulled herself away from the celebration and stepped in front of him. "Are you angry, Abba?"

"No." He shook his head. "I'm not angry. I

simply want the best for you."

"And you're not sure Timothy is such?"

He looked up at her. "I feel no one would be good enough for you."

She saw the light catch in his moist eyes and embraced him. "Don't worry. Timothy is what's best for me. He will care for me as you do."

"I can only pray that will be true."

"I hope you do," she teased.

Caleb opened his arms wide and folded them around her. "May you know nothing but joy."

"Thank you, Abba."

When she turned back to the group, Timothy was waiting for her.

"I have something for you." He held out a wrapped gift.

Lea accepted it and gently untied the thin twine. A gorgeous piece of material shone bright in her hands. "I don't know what to say. It's beautiful."

"I have to confess, Priscilla helped me choose the fabric." He nodded to the woman over his shoulder.

She bowed.

"Thank you both."

"May it and your ring be a reminder that I will return for you as soon as our betrothal time is complete."

She smiled and pressed the fabric to her chest.

"I will be waiting."

Chapter Ten

"Let him kiss me with the kisses of his mouth: for thy love is better than wine."
-Song of Solomon 1:2

A.D. 55

Lea pulled at the last stitch as she sat in the main area of her home. The light coming in from the open window was perfect to see the details she had added to the garment.

"It was fine yesterday." Her mother stood over her examining the dress.

"It's even better today."

"Your sewing skills certainly have improved over the last few months."

"These twelve months have been the longest of my life." She held the dress up to inspect the fine details.

"Think how poor Timothy must feel." Kelilah giggled.

"He's all I've been thinking about."

"Well, I know my opinion doesn't count for much, but I think you're ready to be his wife."

Lea stood and embraced her mother. "Your opinion means everything to me. I don't know what I would have done without yours and Priscilla's constant counsel this past year."

"If that's true, then you'll put that dress away and help your poor old mother in the kitchen."

"Sorry, Ima. I just want it to be perfect."

"I know." She fingered the fabric. "But you need to remember, it's the woman in the dress that makes it right not the stitching. Timothy is going to look right past all this detail to see you. He's not marrying a dress, you know."

"I know." She smiled. "He's marrying me."

She folded the garment as carefully as she could and then wrapped it up. She didn't want even the tiniest grain of dirt to touch the dress.

Kelilah walked with her into the kitchen and handed Lea a spoon to stir the stew.

"You know it's not just that I want the dress to be perfect. Every time I work on it, I think about Timothy and him coming for me."

"That is what a good bride gift does."

"What was Abba's bride gift to you?"

"This." Kelilah touched her necklace. "I wore it from the moment he handed it to me. Every time I wondered if the day would ever come, I'd touch this necklace and remember the promise he made to return for me."

A knock at the front door caught both

women's attention.

Lea slowly turned to her mother and raised an eyebrow.

"Your father will get it," she reassured her.

Lea's heart pounded wildly in her chest.

"She's in the kitchen," Lea heard Caleb tell the visitor.

Footsteps behind her caused Lea to spin around.

Priscilla stood there with a silly grin.

"Oh, it's you."

"You don't sound so happy to see me."

"Forgive me. I was just hoping to see…"

Priscilla chuckled. "Oh, I know exactly who you were hoping to see." She hugged the younger woman tight.

"I know I'm happy to see another pair of female hands," Kelilah joked. "The ones attached to this girl have done nothing but sew."

Lea blushed.

"Where are your other lovely daughters?"

"I sent them out for a few things. They have been under my feet since last week when the betrothal year ended."

"I thought you'd be happy to have all of them back under the same roof again."

"It was nice for the first few days, but now I remember why we married them off."

Priscilla's laughter bounced around the room.

"I'm sure it won't be much longer. What can I help with?"

Kelilah pointed out some items that needed chopping and set her guest to work.

Lea turned back to the stew on the fire and mindlessly stirred. Her thoughts were on the broad smile of a man she hadn't seen in days.

The sound of the front door opening almost sent Lea running to it. She gripped the spoon with both hands and tried to ignore the interruption.

Priscilla patted her shoulder.

"I don't know how much longer I can keep up like this," Lea whispered.

"We have returned," Zahara announced as she placed an armful of items on the counter.

The two younger sisters followed with piles of food.

"How are you holding up?" Nava squeezed Lea's hand.

"She's about to be driven to madness," Kelilah answered for her. "And so am I if things don't calm down."

"Oh, Ima." Zahara shook her head as she sorted the vegetables.

"I remember my wedding day," Nava reminisced. "Seems like it was only yesterday."

"It was barely two years ago," Jerusha said. "And soon your little one will be here." She rubbed her sister's growing midsection.

Lea placed her hand there too. "I'll finally be an aunt again."

"A new bride and a renewed aunt," Priscilla commented. "What a joyous time for you."

Lea turned to Jerusha. "When will you and Reuben give me a baby to squeeze?"

Her sister's cheeks flushed crimson.

"No!"

She nodded. "I wanted to wait until after your marriage feast to tell you, but all this waiting is making me anxious."

"You're expecting?" Kelilah practically sung the question.

Jerusha held out her hands. "Yes, Ima. Are you pleased?"

"Of course." She hugged her daughter. "You know I love nothing more than being a Safta to all my grandchildren."

"When are you going to tell Abba?" Zahara asked.

"Let's wait until after the wedding feast," Kelilah offered. "He has enough on his platter to worry about."

Lea placed a hand on Jerusha's stomach. "Two new lives coming."

"And one getting ready to begin," Priscilla said with a grin.

Lea tilted her head.

A loud sound came from outside.

Zahara stepped toward the main area. "Is that a—"

"Shofar." Lea recognized the sound immediately. Her ears had been listening for nothing else.

Her sisters fled toward the door.

She turned toward her mother and Priscilla.

They both nodded.

"You'd better go," Priscilla suggested.

Lea made it to the open door just in time to hear the words she had been longing for echo down the street.

Tychicus, dressed in splendor, rounded the corner shouting, "Behold, the bridegroom comes."

Paul, matched in garments, blew the shofar beside him.

They came to the bottom of the steps.

"Paul, you have news to share?" Caleb asked, standing in front of his daughters.

"As father to Timothy, I have thoroughly inspected the place he is to take his bride. It is a more than suitable dwelling. He has been under my and Aquila's teaching concerning marriage and we have both agreed he is ready."

Tychicus stepped toward them. "Lea, do you understand what Paul's trying to say?"

She nodded.

"I've come to prepare the way. Timothy is

ready to take you as his bride."

Her head spun and she forgot how to breathe. "Timothy?" The name tasted sweet on her lips. "He's coming?"

"Yes." His entire face lit up. "He's coming for you. Are you ready?"

"Of course." She shook away the dizziness.

"It's a good thing an extra pair of hands showed up." Priscilla came up behind her.

Realization dawned on Lea like a bright morning. She glanced over her shoulder. "You knew."

"Perhaps." She shrugged. "You are speaking to Timothy's temporary mother."

Lea put her hands on her hip and shook her head. "Were you planning on telling me?"

"I much prefer that look of surprise on your face." She winked.

She opened her mouth to give her a hard time, but her father interrupted the banter.

"It's time to make our way to the synagogue," Caleb ordered.

Tychicus turned back to the street and continued shouting his line. Musicians proceeded along the way playing jubilant music.

Lea stretched toward the crowd that lined the street desperate to catch a glimpse of Timothy.

"Not a moment to spare." Kelilah pushed Lea into the house. "We need to get you dressed for your bridegroom."

The next moments became a blur as Lea was passed from one set of hands to the next. Her sister, mother, and dearest friend cleansed her skin, dressed her in the garment she had taken a year to sew, brushed and pinned her hair, and decorated her in lavish ornaments. The final piece was a sheer cloth draped over her.

"You're as beautiful as Rebekah." Kelilah wiped her damp eyes.

When Lea could remain still no longer, the women took up their lamps and led the way outside. At the bottom of the steps, Caleb stood with the other elders. She met him there.

Caleb took her hand. "I have the great honor of once again taking my role as father and Rabbi to escort you to your bridegroom."

"I'm ready."

They followed a band of the musicians and lamp carriers down the street toward the synagogue.

At the opening, Timothy stood with Tychicus and Aquila on either side.

Lea couldn't take her eyes off him. He was decorated as elaborately as she, but she looked past all that to the happiness that radiated off his face. It was like a beacon calling her home.

When she neared him, Timothy raised her veil. "Just making sure they haven't switched you with one of your sisters," he teased and let the material fall back into place.

"I'm the last one left," she joked.

He stretched out his hand to her.

Caleb offered her to him.

Lea felt the heat rise in her cheeks when their skin touched. It was a welcoming warmth that she never wanted to end.

Coins and grains rained down on them from the hands of those gathered.

"He makes peace in your borders. He fills you with the finest of wheat," the crowd shouted. "Be fruitful and multiply."

Lea snickered as she watched grains stick in Timothy's hair.

"Almost makes me wish I were the one wearing a veil." He winked.

Lea was happy the covering protected her from the downpour of favor.

Timothy released her hand, but not before giving it a gentle squeeze. He stepped inside the synagogue.

Lea waited for the musicians to go ahead of her and followed them inside. Her eyes quickly found her bridegroom seated on the bench on the raised platform.

She took her place on his right side and Priscilla and Kelilah came to stand behind her.

Timothy took her hand again.

The warmth flooded her afresh and she smiled in spite of herself.

Caleb stood in front of the couple and removed his prayer shawl. He laid it carefully over them.

He took a cup of wine and prayed, "Blessed are You, Adonai our God, Sovereign of all, Creator of the fruit of the vine."

Timothy and Lea each took a sip from the cup.

Rabbi Caleb offered prayers of blessing over their union and praise for the joyous time Yahweh had seen fit to provide. Then he removed his prayer shawl from their heads.

"Ready?" Tychicus appeared at Timothy's side.

He nodded and rose. "I'll see you soon," he promised Lea.

"My sisters will have to restrain me."

He laughed and left with his group of men.

"I don't think we have to give him too much of a head start," Priscilla commented. "He probably ran all the way there."

Lea giggled. She imagined her new husband sprinting all the way to the home they would share.

"Shall we?" She held out her hand. "Let's not keep that bridegroom of yours waiting too long."

"He kept me waiting long enough. If only I had the will to let him stew for a while."

"You will have the rest of your life to repay him for making you wait."

Lea thought on that idea. "You're right. I'm ready to go."

Her mother and Timothy's surrogate mother led her and her sisters up the street.

"Where are we going?" Lea asked impatiently.

"We're almost there," Priscilla assured her.

When they reached the door where Timothy stood, Lea turned to Priscilla. "Here?"

She nodded.

"We can't take your home."

"No one is taking anything." She put her hands on her broad hips. "Besides, this home doesn't belong to Aquila and me anyway. It's the property of Onesiphorus. We've only been renting since we arrived. It was Paul's idea to have you set up home here."

"She spends most of her time here anyway," Paul mocked. "Might as well make it her home too."

She hugged him. "Thank you."

"You're welcome, young one." He returned the firm embrace. "Now you better get over there to your bridegroom or he is going to come snatch you."

Lea walked over to Timothy who stood in the open doorway.

"I've been waiting for you," he said.

"Not as long as I've been waiting for you."

He reached for her hand and placed it on the upper post. "You are now the mistress of this house." Without looking back, he ushered her inside and shut the door on the crowd.

Lea listened to the group leave.

"And now, Lea bat-Caleb, it's finally time for us." His eyes shone with a hint of hunger.

They only had a short time together before the procession of people returned to escort them to Rabbi Caleb's home for the first night of feasting.

For seven nights, they rejoiced with everyone who showed up for food and fellowship in the different homes who welcomed them.

At the synagogue on the following Sabbath, Lea sat next to her new husband and friends who were closer than family. Her mother smiled at her from her place across the room.

After the official start to the meeting, Rabbi Caleb made his way to the raised platform and unrolled the scroll.

"I have the unique honor of reading today from one of my favorite places. In celebration of my youngest daughter's marriage, I will be reading the story of Isaac's marriage."

Caleb bowed his head and read, " 'Then I bowed my head and worshiped the Lord and blessed the Lord, the God of my master Abraham, who had led me by the right way to take the daughter of my master's kinsman for his son. Now then, if you are going to show steadfast love and faithfulness to my master, tell me; and if not, tell me, that I may turn to the right hand or to the left.

" 'Then Laban and Bethuel answered and said, "The thing has come from the Lord. We cannot speak to you bad or good. Behold, Rebekah is before you. Take her and go, and let her be the wife of your master's son, as the Lord has spoken." And they called Rebekah and said to her, "Will you go with this man?" She said, "I will go." ' "

Timothy took Lea's hand and gave it a firm squeeze.

" 'So, they sent away Rebekah their sister and her nurse, and Abraham's servant and his men,' " Caleb continued. " 'And they blessed Rebekah and said to her, "Our sister, may you become thousands of ten thousands, and may your offspring possess the gate of those who hate him!"

" 'Then Rebekah and her young women arose and rode on the camels and followed the man. Thus, the servant took Rebekah and went his way.

" 'Now Isaac had returned from Beerlahairoi and was dwelling in the Negeb. And Isaac went out to meditate in the field toward evening. And he lifted up his eyes and saw, and behold, there were camels coming.

" 'And Rebekah lifted up her eyes, and when she saw Isaac, she dismounted from the camel and said to the servant, "Who is that man, walking in the field to meet us?"

" 'The servant said, "It is my master." So, she took her veil and covered herself.

" 'And the servant told Isaac all the things that he had done. Then Isaac brought Rebekah into the tent of Sarah his mother and took her, and she became his wife, and he loved her. So, Isaac was comforted after his mother's death.' "

Lea smiled up at Timothy. Her heart felt as if it were trying to stretch to fill her chest. Her life was peaceful and content. The love of her life sat next to her and laid beside her at night. The people she loved most in the world all sat under the same roof listening to the words of Yahweh together.

Hope burned bright in Lea. She whispered sweet praise to the Savior who made it all possible.

Chapter Eleven

"For this cause have I sent unto you Timotheus, who is my beloved son, and faithful in the Lord, who shall bring you into remembrance of my ways which be in Christ, as I teach every where in every church." – 1 Corinthians 4:17

"You're leaving!" Lea yelled.

"Lower your voice," Timothy demanded.

"We've been married for three months. Now you're telling me you're getting on a boat and I'm supposed to rejoice?"

"You knew this was eventually going to happen."

She folded her arms across her body. "I didn't think it would be so soon."

"We've been preparing for more than a year. Paul wants me to take a letter to Corinth before he arrives."

"And I'm to remain here and wait for whenever Paul decides to let you return?"

He walked across the room they shared in the rented house and kissed the top of her head. "You knew I was a traveler before we were betrothed."

"I assumed I'd be going with you."

"Absolutely not."

"But I don't understand—"

"It's far too dangerous for you."

"Yahweh will protect me as He has you."

"I won't hear of it." He stormed out of the room.

Lea sat on their bed not knowing whether to scream or cry or both. She wiped her face with her hands and held her palms on her cheeks.

An idea struck like lightning. She searched through her belongings and found something that could change Timothy's mind.

Stepping gently into the hallway, she searched for her husband. He was nowhere to be found. The kitchen was empty, but the main area was not. Paul sat with his parchments spread in front of him. An even wilder idea took root inside her. She clutched her hope to her chest and walked over to Paul.

"If you're looking for your husband, he left."

Lea dropped her money pouch on the table in front of him.

Paul looked up from his writing and back down again. "May I help you, young one?"

"This is for you."

"I can't accept it."

"Do you know what it is?"

"It's part of the bride price we paid. Your

father's gift to you."

"As such, it is mine to do with what I wish, is it not?"

Paul set down his quill. "It was used to purchase you."

"As my property, I'm choosing to use it to profit the Way."

"And what of your future?"

"Timothy is my future. Whatever Yahweh has called him to do, as his partner, I should do my best to help him accomplish it."

"I see."

"I do have one request."

"This offering comes with conditions?"

"No." She cooled. "The money is yours to use for the mission whether you grant my request or not."

"Speak on then."

"I wish to go with him."

"Out of the question."

"I believe I can be of help."

"You've never been to Corinth or even outside of Ephesus for that matter. Travel alone can be dangerous. Carrying the message of the Way adds more layers of risk. We never know what may happen."

"That's what Timothy said." Lea sat down across from him. "Yahweh put a longing in my heart to go. Please help me follow that path."

"What about Timothy?"

"What about him?"

"He is your husband and if he has forbidden you…"

"You are his teacher, father figure, and leader of these journeys. He'll do as you ask if you grant me permission."

"Let me think on this matter and I will have an answer for you soon."

She rose. "Thank you."

When she made it back to her room, she spent the next hour praying that Yahweh would soften not only Paul's heart but her husband's. She also asked for His peace regardless of their decision.

Everyone was quiet during the evening meal. Lea figured out word had spread through the house of her earlier disagreement with Timothy.

As Priscilla and Lea cleared the table, Paul finally spoke, "Could everyone please be seated?"

Aquila exchanged a curious glance with his wife who simply shrugged and sat.

Lea didn't have to look at her husband. She knew what Paul wanted to deliberate with the group. Her only hope was that the others would be on her side.

"There is a matter with the upcoming journey we need to discuss."

"Is there a problem with the finances?" Aquila asked.

"No," Paul assured him. "In fact, due to an anonymous donor, our funds have only increased."

Lea fought down the heat rising in her cheeks. She kept her gaze on her folded hands in her lap.

"Praise Yahweh," Priscilla said.

"Indeed." Paul adjusted in his seat. "I fear I have a rather unusual request that has been brought to my attention."

Lea dared a short peek at her husband whose intent focus was on Paul.

"We have someone who wishes to join the mission to Corinth with Timothy and Erastus."

"How wonderful," Aquila said. "More feet to bring the message."

"Well," Paul struggled. "The request is an unusual one."

"You've said that," Aquila commented. "What is so unusual?"

"It's unusual in the fact that it is our young Lea here who wishes to go."

Timothy stood abruptly and faced the door.

"Sit," Paul commanded.

Lea watched Timothy's shoulders heave a few times before he turned back around and obeyed.

He refused to look at her.

"I've prayed on this matter." Paul kept his focus on Timothy. "I ask that everyone here spend time praying on it as well."

"I see no reason why she can't go."

"Hold your tongue, Wife," Aquila ordered.

"I will not." Priscilla slapped the table. "Paul called this meeting with all of us and I'm sure he wants to hear from all of us."

"It's true, old friend." Paul put a firm hand on Aquila's shoulder. "I do want to hear from everyone. Lea is part of this family now."

Lea looked longingly at Aquila.

Priscilla was the one to speak, "Again I say, what issue is there with her joining her husband? I've spent every moment by your side, Husband."

"Because we were forced out of our home," Aquila said. "We didn't have a choice. Lea does."

"And she's choosing to be a help meet for Timothy. Why should she be hindered?"

"It's not safe."

"Nowhere is safe anymore."

"I'm afraid you're both right," Paul interjected. "Lea, if you went to Corinth, I couldn't guarantee your protection."

It was Timothy's turn to protest with a pound of his fist on the table. "I don't see why we are even discussing this as if it were an option."

"Lea is not only part of this family, but a follower of the Way," Paul reminded him. "It is every followers' responsibility to spread the message."

"Which she can do from here in Ephesus."

Paul sighed and moved to sit next to Timothy. "Son, you've chosen a bride who desires the same things you do. She desperately wants to follow Yahweh's path for her life and she believes that path is by your side. I can't fault her for that."

"As her husband, I have forbidden it."

Paul wrapped his short arm around the younger man's back. "I know you're scared…"

Timothy finally looked up to meet his gaze. "It's my job to protect her."

"No, Son, it's not. That's Yahweh's job. Your duty is to love her."

"How can I love her and knowingly place her in danger?"

"I think our Yahweh can handle protecting one more." He attempted a smile, but it didn't reach his eyes.

"Is this your final say?"

Paul looked to Lea. "I wish to hear from everyone this involves."

"I want to go," Lea said softly.

"I think she should," Priscila agreed.

Aquila shook his head. "Though danger faces us at every turn, if Yahweh has called her to go, we shouldn't stop her."

Paul turned to Timothy. "You've heard the wise counsel of those who care for you both. I too believe she should go if it is her desire."

"Then my say doesn't matter."

"Your say carries more weight than us all. I think you should seek Yahweh's face on this."

"And what of Erastus?" Aquila asked. "Does he get a say on the matter?"

"He should be here in a few days. We will ask him when he arrives."

"Then I will hold my final say until we speak with him," Timothy answered.

The next three days were quiet torture for Lea. Timothy was polite, but distant. The others gave her knowing glances and encouraging touches. Still, it wasn't enough to settle the unease she felt in her husband's presence. Every spare moment she poured her heart out before Yahweh.

After visiting her sisters, Lea spent the rest of the late part of the morning people watching by the bay. She didn't want to say anything to her family until the final plans were resolved.

When a ship unloaded and a man matching Priscilla's description of Erastus stepped off, her heart raced. Her thoughts were confirmed when she witnessed Paul welcome the man. The two faced toward the rented house and she followed them.

The mid-day break was coming upon them, so Lea knew Priscilla and Aquila would soon follow. It was the perfect time for a meeting to catch Erastus up on the plans.

After a filling meal, Paul once again requested

the entire household join him at the table.

"Now that Erastus has joined us, we can finalize our plans for Corinth," Paul said.

"I was sure you'd have confirmed everything by now," Erastus mentioned curiously.

"It seems we have one last thing to settle. The group has elected to wait until your arrival in order to give you a chance to speak on the matter."

"Oh?" His bushy eyebrows nearly jumped off his forehead.

"You see, since we last spoke, our Timothy here has married."

"Congratulations." He slapped Timothy on the back. "Who is the favored young lady?"

"Our young Lea bat-Caleb." Paul waved toward her.

"Congratulations, my dear. You've caught a fine catch. Timothy is a most upstanding man." His grin was almost as broad as Timothy's used to be.

She smiled sheepishly.

"You see, friend," Paul explained. "It is Lea whom we must discuss."

"I don't understand." He glanced between the couple.

"Lea has requested to join you and Timothy back to Corinth in order to help support her husband on this journey."

"I see." He rubbed his bearded chin. "And you

are protesting such a request?"

"Not I," Paul said. "Her husband."

"Timothy?" He faced the younger man. "I'm astonished that you would refuse your lovely bride anything."

Lea's estimation of this new friend went up a few notches. He reminded her of her father. Both men were like wheat. If one could make it past the rough chaff exterior, they would find the kernels of nourishment inside.

Timothy kept his head lowered. "I wish to protect my wife from harm."

"So, the decision is mine?" he wondered.

"No," Paul said. "Timothy has the final say of his wife's path, but he is withholding his final judgment until we hear your opinion."

"And the rest of you?"

"We've all agreed to allow her to remain by her husband's side."

Erastus tapped his finger on his chin a few times. "It would be my honor to travel with the bride Timothy has chosen. I will do my best to make sure she is cared for in my city."

Paul reached over and placed his hand on Timothy's arm. "What say you?"

He looked up into the deep eyes of his mentor. "She may go."

Lea wished she could rejoice, but the look of defeat on her husband's face cut through her heart like a knife through goat cheese.

"Then the matter is settled and we can move forward with our plans. Timothy, Erastus, and Lea will go ahead to Corinth to begin a collection for the poor in Jerusalem and give notice of my impending visit." Paul rose, indicating the others could leave as well.

Timothy stood and made his way to the back of the house.

"Come, Erastus," Paul offered. "I want to show you the school I've been teaching at for the past few years. I must inform Tyrannus that my use of his generous offer is about to expire."

Lea sat next to Priscilla watching the hallway.

"He'll come around," her friend promised.

"I hope so," Lea agreed, but lifted a prayer to Yahweh none the less on behalf of her husband.

Chapter Twelve

"And ye are puffed up, and have not rather mourned, that he that hath done this deed might be taken away from among you."
-1 Corinthians 5:2

Lea stood between Timothy and Erastus at the bottom of the boat ramp. She gave another tight embrace to Priscilla and Aquila. She burned their faces into her memory creating strength to draw upon for whatever faced her.

Paul passed a scroll into Timothy's hands. "Be brave, my son. I expect to greet our fellow believers upon your return."

The trio boarded the ship and set sail for Corinth.

Lea stood on the deck of the boat for much of the trip. Her stomach tossed with the waves, but the joy of obedience held her meager meals in place. The advice of the captain to keep her eyes on the horizon also helped.

Timothy stood next to her and wrapped an arm around her waist.

She laid her head on his chest. "Will your

anger towards me ever cool?"

"I'm not angry that you wish to obey Yahweh. I only want you to be safe."

"You told me a year ago that Yahweh called me 'bringer of good news.' And yet you, like my father, wish to keep me bound to one city."

Timothy stared out over the water. "I did say that didn't I?" He kissed her forehead.

"Does that mean you're no longer upset?"

He hugged her tighter to himself. "I love you and only want the best for you, but I can't ignore what Yahweh has called you to do. Maybe He will use you in Corinth in a way He couldn't use me."

Lea closed her eyes and tried to imagine the city she hadn't seen yet, but would be viewing in a short number of days. She whispered a prayer that Yahweh would see fit to use her in some small way.

When her sandaled toes touched the dock at Corinth, Lea's heart skipped a few beats. The grandeur of the city reminded her of her home town, but the city of Corinth could fit a few of her Ephesus within its borders. The buildings seemed to go on forever.

"Welcome to Corinth," Erastus said with a grin. "Land of possibilities."

"Let's just hope Paul's letter guarantees a warm welcome." Timothy patted his shoulder bag.

"That letter and me." He winked. "Let's get

you two to your quarters. I'm sure you could do with a few moments to clean up before we see the elders."

"So soon?" Timothy asked.

"Of course. They are expecting you."

Lea followed the men through the winding streets of Corinth. She stuck as close to Erastus as she could manage. If she were to take her eyes off him, she was sure she'd be lost for weeks.

When her feet ached, Erastus finally turned them into a courtyard. An elaborate fountain standing between two lavish gardens welcomed them. The fountain poured into a round pool. Lea leaned over to peer inside. Large bass swam freely in the clear water.

The house was twice the size of her family's villa and nearly that size over again of the rented home she shared with four others and whoever was visiting Ephesus. Lea was overwhelmed at the size of the house belonging to her new friend.

Erastus watched her reaction and chuckled. "I suppose being Corinth's chief treasurer does have its advantages." He glanced over his house. "Please make yourselves comfortable. For the duration of your stay, my home is your home."

"We are grateful for your hospitality," Timothy said.

"Faunus," Erastus' deep voice carried through the vast space.

A man seemed to appear from the air. "Master, it's good to see you've returned." He bowed deeply.

"Good to be home." He put his arm around his servant's shoulder. "This is Faunus, my most faithful servant. Anything you need, simply call for him." He waved to the couple. "These are Paul's friends, Timothy and his wife, Lea. Make them feel at home."

"It would be my pleasure, Master."

"Good." He rubbed his hands together. "Show them the guest room upstairs while I go see to my wife."

"She was in the outer courtyard a few moments ago."

"Thank you, Faunus. I'll collect you two shortly." He walked toward the back of the house.

"Follow me, please." The servant led them up a set of stairs to the second story. "Your room is right this way." He waved to an open door. "If there is anything you need, simply let me know." He bowed and took his leave.

Lea walked the length of the spacious room. "This is twice the size of the room we share in Ephesus." She pressed on the mattress. "It's so inviting. Do you think we have time for a short nap?"

Timothy shook his head. "Erastus will return soon. We need to be ready to meet the elders of the churches."

She bit her lip. "I must admit I'm nervous."

"You're not the only one."

"What do you have to be nervous over? You've traveled with Paul for so long. This is my first time doing anything like this."

"It's been a while since I've been here. I spent a lot of time traveling back and forth from here to Thessalonica. Mostly I was an encourager. It's a different duty all together to be a representative. Especially since I know what this letter holds."

"You don't think they will welcome the words?"

Timothy sighed. "Paul added in a few lines of recommendation for me. Let's hope they help."

"Hope can be a powerful thing," she reminded him.

The two set to work removing the salty air and boat grime from themselves and donning fresh clothes.

Erastus retrieved them as promised and escorted them to the gathering of the elders.

"This is Benjamin's home," Erastus explained as they walked the path to the large house. "He is the chief elder and has offered the space as their meeting place."

"I don't remember him."

"There have been many changes since you last visited."

A shiver ran down Lea's back at his words. She didn't know if they were meant as a warning, but she couldn't help but take them as such.

The spacious meeting place was filled with older Jewish men. Erastus greeted the elders and introduced them to Timothy and Lea.

Halfway through the introductions, Lea had a difficult time remembering the first person's name and by the end had forgotten all of them. She put on a smile and attempted to blend into the stone walls. The soft bed of Erastus' guest room was becoming even more tempting. She wished she had remained there. It was becoming clear to her that there was no possible way she could be anything but a hindrance here.

Timothy handed the scroll to Benjamin. "I've come to read this to your churches."

The older man unrolled the scroll. His eyes darted right to left over the parchment. When he was finished, he looked Timothy up and down. "We don't need a boy to tell us how to run our meetings." He rolled up the letter and handed it back to Timothy.

The younger man took the scroll and returned it to his bag. "I speak on behalf of Paul."

"Why isn't Paul here himself instead of sending us a youth?" a man from the side called out.

"I can assure you all, I've spent a great deal of

time under Paul's teaching. He has given me his authority to speak to you. At this time, he is preparing for a trip to Macedonia himself. He simply sent me here to help with some of the difficulties you seem to be having and to collect funds for the poor in Jerusalem."

"Difficulties?" Another gray-bearded man asked. "What difficulties?"

"Paul wishes to address these issues in the public setting of your meeting."

"He only wants our money for himself."

"Paul works by his own hands to support his missions. But even if he didn't, it is the duty of the church to support his work and those that assist in that endeavor."

"What of your pretty young wife there?" Benjamin wagged his boney finger at Lea. "Are we supporting her as well?"

"She is part of our body of believers and has dedicated her life in service just like the rest of us."

"You should be supporting her instead of coming here to scold us as if we are children."

"That was not my intent. I'm merely here to read Paul's letter and help you on your path to repentance."

"Repentance?" the oldest huffed.

"For example, you have a man in your flock who is living in open fornication with his father's wife and you've done nothing about it."

Lea's heart hurt. She didn't know these people, but it was painfully obvious their sins were causing issues among their group. Paul was right; she wasn't prepared for such a journey.

"They are not hurting anyone," another man explained.

"Only themselves and every believer you have here," Timothy answered. "Their actions are a testimony to what you allow."

"We should have the say in what we allow." Benjamin set his shoulders back.

"I'm bound to fulfill my duty to Paul and deliver this letter as he has ordered. Respectfully, I request you listen to its message and take it to heart."

Benjamin opened his mouth to speak, but Erastus beat him to it. "I believe that's enough for now."

Lea wanted to hug the man for rescuing them from further torment.

"Let's all get a good night's sleep. The morning light will shine a fresh perspective on these issues." He placed a hand on Timothy's back. "Let's go," he whispered.

"I thank you for your time," Timothy said with a bow.

"Erastus, maybe you can treat your guests to a bedtime tale."

Lea didn't see where the comment came from

as many of the men joined in the laughter. She turned her back on them and followed her husband out.

"I've never been so insulted in all my life," Timothy fumed.

"Forgive their pride. They believe themselves to be chief in all matters, but especially their churches."

"I'm here because Paul sent me. It is not of my own arrogance and righteousness."

"I understand that. We simply need to make them see."

"Maybe I should visit with her," Lea suggested.

Erastus glanced at Timothy. "Who?"

"The woman that was spoken of."

"I don't think that's a good idea," Timothy said.

"I don't see where a visit would hurt," Erastus offered. "I don't think she could fall deeper into sin."

"Only if your wife goes with her."

"I'll arrange it for after the meetings tomorrow."

The following morning, Lea sat among a large group of believers.

Erastus introduced Timothy and welcomed him to read Paul's letter.

Timothy cleared his throat, unrolled the

scroll, and began reading.

Upon hearing the letter, Lea understood Timothy's fear. Some of the words were encouraging, but most of them were correcting and calling out of church issues.

The flock didn't respond well to the public exposure of their sins. Many times during the reading, people gasped or groaned.

After all day reading the letter to each of the house churches, Timothy came to the end of the letter one more time, " 'The churches of Asia send you greetings. Aquila and Priscilla, together with the church in their house, send you hearty greetings in the Lord.' "

At the mention of her friend's names, Lea almost wept. She missed them terribly and longed for the warm embrace of her motherly companion.

" 'All the brothers send you greetings,' " Timothy continued. " 'Greet one another with a holy kiss. I, Paul, write this greeting with my own hand. If anyone has no love for the Lord, let him be accursed. Our Lord, come! The grace of the Lord Jesus be with you. My love be with you all in Christ Jesus. Amen.' " He rolled up the scroll and grasped it to his chest.

The tension in the room weighed so heavy even Lea could feel it. For the rest of the meeting, she held her breath that none of the men whom she'd met the evening before would speak ill of her husband.

When the group was dismissed, a beautiful woman came to her side. "Lea?"

"Yes?"

"I'm Hadassah, Erastus' wife. He told me you wanted to visit one of our women."

"I would."

"The men wanted to meet with the elders again. So, I'm here to escort you. She has agreed to meet with you at her home."

Lea waved her ahead.

They walked through the busy roads until Hadassah stopped at a house. "Here we are."

Lea carefully removed her sandals and waited as her guide knocked.

An older woman with crimped hair opened the door. "Hadassah, I've been expecting you."

"Valeria, this is Lea. She is Timothy's wife. They are visiting from Ephesus."

"Please come in."

They entered the modest villa. Lea took note of the beautiful mosaics of birds on the walls. The smell of lamb stew wafted from the kitchen and made her stomach growl. She had been escorted from meeting to meeting with Timothy without a chance to eat. She pushed the physical discomfort aside.

"I was hoping to speak to you privately on a

matter," Lea offered.

"I heard the letter." Valeria tightened her lips.

Lea fought the rising lump in her throat that threatened to stop her voice. "I was hoping I could help."

"You think you're the first?" She put a hand on her hip. "Perhaps the youngest. Tell me something. How long have you been married?"

Lea looked to Hadassah then back to her. "Less than a year."

"Barely a year and you believe you have the right to counsel me in my relationship?"

"I don't come in judgment."

"Oh?"

"I've come prayerfully hoping to help resolve the matter."

"That's all well and good for you, but I'm not going to change my mind." She moved deeper into her home toward the kitchen. "My former husband was a man who used me for his gain. The man whom I live with now cares for me."

"You mean your step-son?"

She paused only briefly before returning to the preparations she had been tending to before answering the door. "Seth is a good man."

"Who should not be sharing your bed."

Valeria spun on her heels and waved a spoon in Lea's face. "My business is none of yours. You may see yourself out of my home."

Hadassah stepped between them. "Valeria, please—"

"You can leave as well." She turned her back to them.

"Come, Lea."

Lea walked away in defeat. She stayed behind Hadassah all the way back to her hostess' home.

When the large villa came into view, Timothy was standing outside waiting for them.

"I'll let you speak to him," Hadassah said. "When you're done, I'll serve the mid-day meal."

She nodded.

Timothy searched Lea's face. "How did it go?"

She looked at him through damp eyes. "Valeria wouldn't listen to anything I tried to say. Her sin has her so entangled that she doesn't see how trapped she has become."

"It's not your fault." He pulled her close. "It takes time for Yahweh to break up stony hearts."

She wiped her face on her sleeve. "How did your meeting go?"

"About as well as yours." He attempted a smile.

"Oh no." She hugged him tight. "I'm so sorry."

"At least I accomplished my mission. They have heard the letter. We can only pray Yahweh works in them to move to repentance."

She laid her head on his chest. "You can be

sure I will do that."

"Thank you, my love." He stroked her head.

"For what?"

"For coming along. I don't know what I would do without you here beside me."

She closed her eyes and simply held her husband and allowed him to hold her. When she opened her eyes, a familiar face came into view down the path.

"Tychicus?"

Timothy looked in the direction she faced. "It can't be."

Their friend came near and greeted them.

"It's good to see you." Timothy kissed both cheeks of his fellow laborer. "But we weren't expecting you to join us for another week or more."

"I've just returned from Lystra." Tychicus voice was low and solemn. "I'm sorry to bring word of your father's death."

"No." Timothy took a step back. "It can't be true."

"I went in search of you when I received word from Paul that he had sent you on your mission. It seems I missed you in Ephesus by a few days. I caught the very next boat leaving and sought you here in Corinth."

"And my mother?"

"That is why I came looking for you. Your

mother and grandmother are mourning Hector's death. As followers of the way and Jewesses by birth, I fear they may be in danger of losing their home. They are without protection and rights without your father or you."

"I must go to them at once."

"I figured you might say that so I have secured passage for you as soon as you're ready."

"What about the brethren? Paul has requested Sopater, Aristarchus, Secundus, and Gaius to join us in Ephesus."

"You and your wife can go ahead to Lystra to settle your family matters. When you're done, pick up Gaius in Derbe. I'll collect the others in Thessalonica and we'll meet you in Ephesus."

Timothy agreed and rushed inside to pack their things.

"I guess you get that visit to Lystra after all," Tychicus said to Lea.

"I only wish it were under better circumstances."

Within a matter of hours, they packed their belongings, and boarded a ship. Lea waved to Erastus, Hadassah, and Tychicus who had come to see them off. The group had given them their fondest prayers and well wishes for a safe and speedy journey.

Days felt like mere hours when the boat pulled into the docks at Perge. The two made the long trip inland to Timothy's birthplace.

Lea remained silent in respect for her husband's mourning. She too mourned as they traveled. Her wish to meet Timothy's family was finally happening, but she would not get to see the face of the man who fathered her beloved. Now, she must meet her husband's mother and grandmother in the worst time of their life. What comfort could she offer while healing from a failed mission?

Chapter Thirteen

"A father of the fatherless, and a judge of the widows, is God in his holy habitation."
-Psalm 68:5

Lystra

By the time Lea stepped foot in Lystra, she was exhausted. She couldn't imagine how tired Timothy must be. They had traveled days on a ship and then another couple of days over land, but they finally reached their destination.

She took in the market village. It was not as impressive as Corinth. A stranger like her could walk from one end to the other during a short conversation and not realize they had passed all the town had to offer. Still, this is where her dear husband grew into the man she loved.

Timothy wasted no steps or words in making his way toward his childhood home.

The wooden door creaked open revealing an old woman wearing black sackcloth.

"Timothy," her voice broke. "Oh, Timothy!" She pressed herself into her son's arms and kissed his face all over.

He held her tight. "I'm so sorry I wasn't here."

"You're here now," she comforted. "That's all that matters." She peered around him. "This must be the wife you wrote to us about."

Timothy wrapped his arm around Lea and drew her close. "This is Lea bat-Caleb. Lea, this is my mother, Eunice."

"I'm so devastated for your loss."

She cracked a simple smile. "Thank you. Please come in."

Lea stepped into the tiny home. There were no mosaics to cheer up the stone walls. No lavish rooms flowing one into another. It was even smaller than the rented house back in Ephesus, but felt just as warm and welcoming. She could almost feel the joy it must have contained before its loss of master.

"Safta Lois." Timothy made his way to the older woman sitting on a stool in the simple cooking area. She also wore black sackcloth dress. He knelt in front of her.

"It's good to see you." She wrapped her arms around his neck and wept.

"I've prayed for you every day since I left."

"And I you."

"There is someone I'd like you to meet." He waved his wife over. "This is Lea."

Lea bent down and kissed the woman's cheek.

"The pleasure is all mine. Seems I have you and your daughter to thank for the man I love and his heart for Yahweh."

A soft grin stretched the wrinkles in the old woman's face. "I like her."

"Ima, do you have a garment for me? I'm afraid we were on mission when we heard the news."

"Of course, come with me."

Timothy followed her to the back.

Lea looked to Timothy's grandmother. "Can I fix you something to eat, Safta Lois?"

"That would be wonderful."

She set to work gathering bits of the things she found and handed her a small bowl.

"We've had so many sweet visitors bring offerings."

Lea sat on the floor beside her. "It seems your family is well loved here."

"Oh my, yes." She took a small bite of bread. "People in Lystra must take care of each other."

"I'm sorry I didn't get the chance to visit before…"

She nodded. "Hector was a good man. He was very pleased to hear Timothy had taken a bride."

Timothy came back into the room. He had exchanged his tunic for black sackcloth that he ripped on the left side over his chest.

Lea's heart hurt to see the outside picture of what must be going on inside her husband.

"I've prepared an area for you two while you're visiting," Eunice said.

"We are here for more than a visit," Timothy explained.

"You're going to move back home?" Eunice clasped her hands.

Timothy looked to Lea and then back at his mother. "No. I've come to settle Father's estate and make plans for the two of you."

Eunice moved to put her hands on her mother's shoulder. "We'll be fine."

"No, you won't." He walked over to her and held her hand. "Tychicus told me everything. With Father gone, there is nothing to support you."

"You are far too busy to worry about two old women."

"You're my Ima and Safta. It is my responsibility to take care of you."

"What does that mean?"

"I want to move you to our home in Ephesus."

"But you just said you were on mission."

"We were, but we have settled in Ephesus. Paul has a rented house there that we all share."

"All?"

"Myself and Lea, Paul, his fellow tentmakers Aquila and Priscilla, and an occasional visitor or two."

"Sounds full already."

"Paul is planning a trip to Macedonia soon and many more places after that. He'll be gone for a while. Aquila and his wife wish to move back to Rome when the time is right. That simply leaves Lea and me."

"And what if you're sent away again?"

"I'll speak to Paul. I'm sure we can work something out." He held her hand to his chest over the rip. "I want to make sure you're safe. Please?"

"Leave our home and everyone we know?"

"I know it won't be easy," Lea offered. "But I have lots of family in Ephesus and I belong to your family now. It would be a pleasure to have you under our roof. If we left you both here, Timothy would do nothing but worry."

Eunice looked down to her mother. "Let us pray on it."

For the next few days, Timothy was gone from the house setting things in order.

Lea spent her days next to her in-laws hearing stories of Timothy's youth and lending a helping hand.

"Did you come to the Way through Paul?" Lea asked as she kneaded some dough.

"Yes." Eunice wiped her brow. "My family was

Jewish, but there are not many of us here in Lystra. We don't even have a synagogue close by. When Paul came to town preaching about Jesus and performing all kinds of healings, it certainly got our attention."

"He has that way about him," Lea agreed.

"Of course, the Greeks here were convinced him and Barnabas were Hermes and Zeus."

"Really?"

"There is a temple dedicated to Zeus nearby and the priests offered sacrifices to them as if they were the gods themselves."

"What did Paul do?"

"He set them straight right away."

"Did it work?"

"Not really." She shrugged. "People kept offering sacrifices to them. But then some Jews from Antioch and Iconium came and dragged Paul out of the city. They stoned him and left him for dead."

"Oh!"

"Paul defied them all by getting up and coming right back into the city."

"That must have been a sight."

"You can believe if the people didn't think they were gods before they sure did after that."

"Then what happened?"

"They left and went to Derbe, I believe. They came back after a while and encouraged those of us who had believed. Paul appointed two of the men to be elders of our small church. We still meet even though there aren't many of us."

"How old was Timothy?"

"Only a boy then. When Paul came back many years later, he heard about Timothy preaching what we had taught him."

Lea smiled. She could imagine her young husband spreading news about the Way through the small area.

"Paul had just separated from Barnabus at the time. He was looking for a new apprentice."

"I didn't know that."

"Seems they disagreed over a young man named John Mark."

"I know him. He was brought to Ephesus after Barnabus was murdered. Priscilla mentioned he was one of their companions, but not that they had parted paths over a disagreement."

"Paul didn't believe John Mark was committed enough to the Way. He had failed Paul in the past."

"So Barnabus took him?"

"It's easy to understand why. John Mark is Barnabus' cousin. He must have felt obligated to the boy."

"That must have been difficult for them both."

"In a way, yes, but it was for the best."

"How could their division be for the best?"

"Think about it. There have been numerous times in our history in which Yahweh divided us so that we were forced to spread. With Barnabus parting with John Mark at his side the one group of three men became two groups of two men. They could cover twice as much area.

"Timothy was also afforded the opportunity to be a student to the chief spreader of the Way. The things he has seen and been taught would not have happened if Paul kept John Mark under his wing instead."

"I didn't think about it like that."

"Yahweh never wastes moments that He can use."

"You feel moving to Ephesus would be a waste?" Lea wondered.

Eunice stopped. "I hadn't considered that."

"Would you?"

She picked up her preparations. "I don't think you know what you're asking."

"I'm the youngest of four sisters. The people I have shared a home with since being married are making plans to leave and I don't know if I will ever see them again. If Paul sends Timothy away, I'll be residing in an empty house. I don't think I was made for such a task. And I discovered recently that I was not made to…" Tears streamed down her face. "I'm sorry."

Eunice placed a hand on her shoulder. "What

is it?"

"Let's just say the mission Timothy spoke of before our arrival here didn't go as either of us planned."

"Life often doesn't." She took Lea's hand and led her to the table. "Tell me what happened."

Lea wiped her face, but the tears kept coming. "Ever since I could remember, I've wanted to travel. To see the world and everything Yahweh had created." She sniffled. "Timothy and I had only been married a few months when Paul was ready to send him to Corinth. They had received word that the churches there were having some issues that needed to be addressed. Paul wasn't ready to leave yet, so he sent Timothy with Erastus."

Eunice nodded along as Lea spoke.

"I begged them to let me go. I thought I could help."

"Had you prayed about it?"

"Every day." She wiped her face again. "I honestly believed it was the path I was supposed to walk."

"So, what happened in Corinth?"

"Timothy met with the elders and they were so prideful. They were less than welcoming toward us both. Then when the following meeting came, Timothy read the letter Paul had written. The churches didn't accept it as well as we had hoped."

"I see."

"I even went to see the woman involved in one of the issues, but she wouldn't even listen to me. She threw me out of her house without letting me counsel her."

Eunice patted Lea's arm. "That does sound rough."

"Was I wrong to go?" Lea asked. "My presence seemed to only bring contempt for the mission and my words didn't help calm the issue at all. I failed him."

"I don't think Timothy believes that."

"We haven't even had a chance to speak about it. When I came back from my meeting with the woman, Tychicus had found us and gave us the news of Hector's death. We were on a ship before sundown. I wanted to respect Timothy's silence on the journey here. He was grieving so heavily."

"My poor son." Her own tears started. "His heart must be so broken over all this."

"It showed me that I wasn't meant to be by his side on these missions. I was obviously mistaken."

Eunice dried her damp eyes. "You believe you heard Yahweh wrong?"

Lea thought for several moments. "No. My path was as clear as I've ever known anything."

"Then you must trust that Yahweh won't waste your obedience. He sees things very differently than we do. There must be something that He did through you."

"At least I was able to be here for all of you during this time."

She hugged her neck. "We are happy to have you with us."

Within a few days, Eunice and Lois had agreed to move and packed their meager belongings. Timothy settled his family's affairs, sold his family's home, and the four journeyed southeast to collect Gaius in Derbe. From there, Timothy purchased passage for them to return to Ephesus.

Lea held the arm of Safta Lois as they boarded the boat bound for Ephesus. In a few short days across the sea, she would see her beloved city. In her heart, she wished to never leave it again. From the moment she had boarded her first boat, she knew nothing but opposition and heartache. Surely, returning to her home would set things in order.

Chapter Fourteen

"For a certain man named Demetrius, a silversmith, which made silver shrines for Diana, brought no small gain unto the craftsmen;"
-Acts 19:24

Ephesus

The rented house felt even smaller with the increase of bodies. Tychicus had returned with Sopater, Aristarchus, and Secundus. Lea and Timothy had brought back Lois, Eunice, and Gaius. Upon their arrival, they also found Titus had arrived in Ephesus while they were gone.

"Isn't there any way to rent another house for a while?" Lea asked Timothy in the precious few moments they had alone.

"Paul doesn't want to waste funds on such a temporary problem. The group will be leaving soon."

Though she loved the people gathered under the roof, it was growing stifling by the day to constantly be surrounded by bodies.

"What about my father's house?" she offered.

"There is plenty of room there."

"I'll speak to Paul after we send off Titus."

"When does his ship leave?"

"Soon. We need to get down to the docks if we are going to see him off."

Lea switched her garments and prepared to have at least one less body under the same roof.

At the docks, the group prayed over Titus and offered last minute embraces.

Paul handed him a letter to the Corinthians. "We shall see each other again soon."

Timothy stood behind them.

Titus reached for him and embraced him.

"I'm sorry," Lea heard Timothy whisper in Titus' ear.

"Don't worry, brother," Titus whispered back. "All will be set right."

Titus leaned down and kissed Lea on the cheek. "Keep him in line," he joked.

She nodded. "Safe travels."

Titus threw his bag over his shoulder and boarded the boat bound for Corinth.

The group made their way to the Agora to make a few purchases before heading home.

"You two don't speak much of Corinth," Priscilla said as she and Lea browsed some fabrics.

"It was not as successful as Timothy would have wanted."

She held up a tunic to inspect it's worth. "How

do you like your in-laws?"

"They are such sweet women. I'm happy to have them here. Sad about the circumstances, but still they bring my heart joy. Though I will be glad when we have more elbow room."

Priscilla chuckled. "Paul likes to pack them in, uh?" She folded the tunic and returned it to its pile.

"I know it's only for a season. I'm trying to be thankful."

"Speaking of seasons…" she hesitated.

Lea dropped the dress in her hand. "Yes?"

"Aquila and I have been speaking. We feel it's time to go home."

"I was just glancing around. If we need to go home, I'm done." She turned to leave.

"No." Priscilla grabbed her arm. "I mean home to Rome."

"Oh." Lea looked down. "I see."

Priscilla hugged her tight. "I felt the need to tell you first before we announce it to everyone else. We have been finalizing our plans and hope to leave soon."

"How soon?"

She tucked a loose strand of hair behind Lea's ear. "Not soon enough for me, but I'm afraid all too soon for you."

Lea fell on her neck and wept. "I don't know what I'm going to do when you leave."

"You'll go on as you always do. You are strong, Lea. You don't need me around."

"But what if I want you?"

Priscila beamed. "I want to stay with you too. You make me feel young and wanted." She shook her head. "But Rome is my home and I want to see it again."

"I understand." She sighed. "I suppose I must try even harder to be thankful during this season."

Priscilla wrapped her arm around Lea. "We both will."

They walked past a growing crowd.

"What do you supposed is going on?" Lea wondered.

"In my experience, nothing good comes from a crowd."

A man was standing on a stool shouting to the people, "Men, you know we gain our wealth from our business. We see and hear in almost all of Asia that this Paul has persuaded and turned a great many people away from our gods. He says, 'gods made by hands are not gods at all.'"

Murmurs darted through the crowd.

"Do you know him?" Priscilla asked.

"Demetrius," Lea answered. She looked over the older man whose face was hardened by fire and bitterness. "A local silversmith who likes to stir up trouble."

"He is not only a danger to our trade,"

Demetrius continued. "But also to the temple of the great goddess Artemis, the one whom all Asia and the world worships. If we let this happen, she may be deposed of her magnificence."

Echoes of fear erupted from the people. They shouted, "Great is Artemis of the Ephesians!"

Lea caught Timothy's eye. "You need to get Paul away from here. Take him to my father's house and hide him," she begged. "I've seen Demetrius stir up a frenzied crowd before."

Timothy pressed his way out of the crowd.

Lea stuck close to Priscilla.

She searched for a way out of the Agora, but the sea of people had filled in around them to hear the man. "We're never going to be able to get through this."

The crowd shouted against each other and bodies pressed everywhere.

Lea thought to herself that she would rather be in her crowded home with peaceful bodies than here in this throng.

"Here are some of his companions." Demetrius pointed to two men.

Lea and Priscilla craned their necks to see Gaius and Aristarchus.

Some men grabbed them and hauled them away.

"Where are they taking them?" Lea asked.

"I don't know, but let's follow so we can make

sure they are not harmed."

The two women let themselves be carried away with the flow of people.

It wasn't long before Lea realized where they were headed. The massive theater came into view. She watched as the horde poured into the entrance ahead. Priscilla stuck close to her as they entered and found a seat at the bottom of the steps. The escalating stairs filled quickly.

Several metalworkers pressed toward the open area in front of the stage with Gaius and Aristarchus.

"Is there any way to stop this madness?" Lea wondered.

"Let's just pray there is no bloodshed today."

A group of Jews came forward as well and a man named Alexander pushed his way to the front of them. Lea knew him to be a copperworker.

He waved his hands in front of the massive audience trying desperately to quiet them.

"We will hear no Jew!" Demetrius shouted. "Great is Artemis of the Ephesians!"

The metalworkers repeated their cry over and over again until it became a chant. The spectators chanted along without pause.

Lea huddled next to Priscilla. Her ears ached with the deafening shouts of praise to a false god.

An hour passed and then a second.

"Does it normally take this long to rouse your

city administrators?" Priscilla tapped her foot with impatience.

"I've seen it take all day." She pressed her hands over her ears to drown out the chanting.

Finally, a clerk appeared on the stage. He raised both arms to silence the crowd.

When the stillness fell heavy, Lea removed her hands. She sighed with relief at the quiet.

"Men of Ephesus," the clerk shouted so that his voice, with the help of the theater structure, reached even those on the top section. "Who is there who does not know that the city of the Ephesians is temple keeper of the great goddess Artemis and of her sacred image that fell from the sky?"

The group on the group started to speak again, but he held up a hand to keep them calm. "Seeing then that these things cannot be denied, you ought to be quiet and do nothing rash. You have brought these men here," he waved to Gaius and Aristarchus, "who are neither sacrilegious nor blasphemers of our goddess."

Demetrius stepped forward, but the clerk raised his palm to him again. "If you, Demetrius, and your fellow craftsman have a complaint against anyone, the courts are open and there sit proconsuls ready to judge these sorts of issues. You are dangerously close to being charged with rioting today." He set his gaze on the man to make sure he had his full attention. "Since there is no cause to justify this commotion, you are dismissed." He waved them off and exited the stage.

Lea and Priscilla waited for Gaius and Aristarchus at the entrance to the theater. The four companions quickly made their way to their rented house before anyone else could be hauled off.

When they arrived, the others stood waiting for news.

"Praise Yahweh," the cry came from their lips as their fellow laborers entered.

"I'll go retrieve Paul," Tychicus offered.

The two men and two women reported the story to the others while they waited.

When everyone had finally gathered together again, they ate a simple meal with grateful hearts and recounted the story to Paul.

Afterward, Aquila stood and motioned for everyone's attention. "My wife and I have decided it's time to return to Rome."

Priscilla squeezed Lea's hand.

"It has been many years since we set foot on the streets of our home. With the ban lifted and the opposition mounting here, we have decided it's time to move on."

Lea let a single tear escape before she took in a deep breath and calmed herself. She realized she was shaking when Priscilla squeezed her hand again.

Paul stood and embraced his friend. "We will see you off with heavy hearts, but joy in our spirits that you shall take the message of the Way with you wherever Yahweh sets your feet."

"I'm grateful for everything." He wiped his face. "I can't express what you've done for us."

Paul patted his back and offered him to sit. "I too would like to speak. There is still the trip back to Macedonia that I've been praying over. I feel it's time to set out as well."

Lea's heart pounded madly.

"As we sent off Titus, I spoke with a few captains and have secured passage for our group to set sail in a few short days." He looked around the room. "Sopater, Aristarchus, Secundus, Gaius, Tychicus, Trophimus, and Timothy will join me."

At the mention of her husband's name, Lea couldn't breathe past the lump rising in her throat.

"We will prepare for an extended trip and meet up with some of our scattered companions."

Lea couldn't listen to anymore. She became too deaf and blind to what was happening around her. Though the possibility of such decisions constantly circled in the back of her mind, now that the order had been spoken, she could no longer deny it. She knew in the depths of her soul she would not be boarding the boat with the men.

Part of her wanted to demand Timothy to stay and part of her was glad her name had not been added to the list. She didn't want to fail her husband or Paul again, but most of all she didn't want to be a stone on someone else's path to the Way.

Later that night, Lea stole away with Priscilla while the rest found places to lay their heads.

"It seems our crowded season is truly coming to a quick end."

Lea couldn't fight back the tears anymore. They caught in the lamplight and she wished them away.

Priscilla wiped her face. "What is it, child?"

"It's not fair." She sniffled. "You get to do life with your husband. I must be separated from mine."

"Dear, sweet one." She wiped her face again. "Iron can only sharpen iron in close contact. He can't do ministry from afar."

"There are still plenty of people here in Ephesus he could minister to."

"But if Yahweh has called him away…"

"It's Paul who has ordered him away."

"Under the Spirit's leading, I'm sure. Our beloved Paul would not make those choices on his own. Perhaps he feels Timothy would benefit from more training. He is still young, you know."

"But he's been under Paul's wing for years. He is ready to fly on his own."

"Have you so easily forgotten Corinth?"

The words stung Lea's heart like a scorpion. "I think about it every day."

"Then you must realize he may truly not be ready yet."

She sighed. "You're right as usual."

Priscilla pulled her in close. "On this issue, I truly wish I wasn't. I can't imagine the pain your soul will feel to see off your husband. I haven't been separated from mine for over twenty years."

She held onto her friend as if it would be the last time.

Lea stood with the large group of people at the bay. She had spent much of the morning crying as she helped each one prepare for their long journey. Though she didn't want their memories to be of her sorrow, she couldn't help think of the long days ahead she would have to face without them.

The men prepared to board their ship first.

"Farewell, young one." Paul kissed the top of her head. "I'll take care of your husband."

Each of the other men kissed her cheek in turn as she wished them a safe journey. Though most she had known only a short time, they had become as close as brothers.

Timothy was last. He stood in front of her holding her hands in his. "It won't be as long as we think. I'm sure I'll be back in your arms before the changing of the seasons."

Lea held to the promise of hope like a drifting sailor who had fallen overboard clinging to a rope someone had thrown him. "Take care of yourself," she whispered.

"Of course." He kissed her deeply and turned to take his place on board.

Lea laid her head on Priscilla's shoulder while they watched the ship sail down the Cayster River. It wasn't until the tiny dot disappeared that she finally looked up to her friend.

"It's time." Priscilla moved to hug her and held her tight. "Who knows, we may see each other in Rome someday."

Lea attempted a smile. Her soul never wanted to climb on another ship again. Yet the promise of another chat in a warm kitchen with Priscilla was almost too tempting to pass up. "Thank you for everything. I shall miss you more than perhaps my husband."

She chuckled. "I might miss you more than mine and he's coming with me."

Aquila wrapped his arms around them both. "I shall not miss your fair city, Lea, but I most certainly will miss you."

Lea snuggled in deep to the loving embrace.

She didn't want the moment to pass. Yet, all too soon it was over and she was waving to the boat carrying her dear friends away. She alone was left standing on the docks.

When she finally made her way home, the streets were less crowded and she realized it was somewhere in the middle of the mid-day break. Her feet dragged down the road and she practically limped home. There would be plenty to do to keep her mind busy, but facing the days with everyone gone would not be easy. Her heart ached and all she wanted to do was cry.

Inside the rented house were Eunice and Lois.

"Is everyone safely on their way?" Eunice asked.

She nodded and made her way to the kitchen to fix some bowls.

"When do we expect them to return?" Lois asked.

Lea set the bowls on the table and sat with a slump. "That's the thing. We don't have any idea of when they will return or if…"

Eunice reached over and patted her hand. "Keep the faith. Yahweh watches over His own."

She looked up into her mother-in-law's face. "I'm trying, but all I honestly feel like doing is curling up until they return."

"Well, we can't have that," Lois said. "We need to keep on living. Just because someone leaves doesn't mean our life stops. We shall see them again soon. When that happens, they need to see that we have remained strong in Yahweh."

She nodded and took a bite of food.

"That's a good girl," Lois encouraged and ate her own food.

The three women sat in silence. Lea took notice of the quiet. The thing she had longed for had now been granted to her. Yet, she would gladly exchange it for the rest of her life for the multitude of bodies of her beloved friends and husband. Tears slipped out and fell into her bowl of stew.

Chapter Fifteen

"For Paul had determined to sail by Ephesus, because he would not spend the time in Asia: for he hasted, if it were possible for him, to be at Jerusalem the day of Pentecost. And from Miletus he sent to Ephesus, and called the elders of the church." -Acts 20:16-17

Months crawled by for Lea. Each day she missed her husband more. No word had been sent about their wellbeing, but she was never promised such.

The house seemed to grow wider every day. Though her days were filled with life advice from her sweet in-laws and work to keep them all fed and cared for, she was desperate for her husband or at least some news of his return.

She adjusted her head wrap and moved to make last-minute adjustments to the main area. It was the Lord's day and soon her home would fill with Way followers.

The first knock at the door started the trickle of believers. With Paul gone, Tyrannus' school was no longer offered as a gathering place. It had become evident to Lea early on that they still needed a dwelling to conduct their weekly meetings. She graciously offered the rented house if only to fill it with life again even if only for a few hours.

When everyone was settled, they broke bread and fellowshipped. The men agreed to take turns every week on who would speak. Some were better orators than others, but all lifted up the name of Jesus as best they could.

Lea was grateful that she could still hold on to the teachings of the Way. She tried to attend synagogue with her parents and sisters as much as she was able, but the time spent there seemed to lack what she found when the Way followers gathered. The same hope and joy in Jesus they shared was the answer she had settled on as to why.

The meeting was coming to a close when a knock interrupted the speaker.

Lea made eye contact with him, then quietly rose to answer it.

Tychicus stood in the doorway. "I come with word from Paul to the elders of the church."

"Come in."

He stood in the middle of the gathering to relay his message. "Paul is in Miletus and is requesting the presence of the elders there."

"Why didn't he come here?" Lea asked.

"He wishes to be in Jerusalem for the day of Pentecost, so he doesn't want to be held here."

"We must go at once," the speaker suggested. "Send word to Paul we will meet him in Miletus."

Tychicus turned to leave.

Lea placed a gentle hand on his arm.

He met her gaze. "He's well and with us in Miletus," he answered her unspoken question. "Come with the elders and see for yourself."

She gave his arm a squeeze of thanks.

He leaned down and kissed her cheek before departing.

Within two days, Lea stood with the elders in Miletus. She insisted on accompanying them to see her husband and none refused her. When she saw Timothy, she fell on his neck and wept. It took longer than she would have liked to compose herself.

Timothy lifted her arms off his shoulders. "Paul is in a hurry."

"I'm just so happy to see you."

"And I you, but Paul has word."

Lea stayed beside her husband clinging to his tunic. If he was leaving again, she was going to soak in every moment.

The men settled around the room.

Paul stood and walked about them. "My heart is overjoyed at seeing all of you. "You yourselves know how I lived among you the whole time from the first day that I set foot in Asia, serving the Lord with all humility and with tears and with trials that happened to me through the plots of the Jews."

He met Lea's glance and smiled. "How I did not shrink from declaring to you anything that was profitable and teaching you in public testifying both to Jews and to Greeks of repentance toward Yahweh and of faith in our Lord Jesus Christ. And now, behold, I am going to Jerusalem, constrained by the Spirit, not knowing what will happen to me there, except that the Holy Spirit testifies to me in every city that imprisonment and afflictions await me."

As he passed, he put his hand on Timothy's shoulder and clasped it. "But I do not account my life of any value nor as precious to myself, if only I may finish my course and the ministry that I received from the Lord Jesus, to testify to the gospel of the grace of Yahweh."

"And now, behold." He moved to stand in front of the room. "I know that none of you among whom I have gone about proclaiming the kingdom will see my face again."

Murmurs and mutters flew around the room.

Lea looked up into Timothy's face, but he held his gaze on his mentor.

Paul held up his arms. "Therefore, I testify to you this day that I am innocent of the blood of all, for I did not shrink from declaring to you the whole counsel of Yahweh. Pay careful attention to yourselves and to all the flock, in which the Holy

Spirit has made you overseers, to care for the church of Yahweh, which He obtained with His own blood."

He put down his arms and hung his head. "I know that after my departure, fierce wolves will come in among you, not sparing the flock. From among your own selves will arise men speaking twisted things, to draw away the disciples after them." He looked up at them.

The men whispered to themselves.

Lea watched Timothy glance out of the corner of his eyes around the room as if searching for the hidden wolf among the sheep. She wanted to ask him what Paul was trying to say, but thought it better to do so in private.

"Therefore, be alert," Paul continued. "Remembering that for three years, I did not cease night or day to admonish every one of you with tears. And now I commend you to Yahweh and to the word of His grace, which is able to build you up and to give you the inheritance among all those who are sanctified. I coveted no one's silver or gold or apparel.

"You yourselves know that these hands ministered to my necessities and to those who were with me." He lifted his hands to his face and then dropped them. "In all things, I have shown you that by working hard in this way we must help the weak and remember the words of the Lord

Jesus, how He Himself said, 'It is more blessed to give than to receive.' It is time for me to continue the path Yahweh has set before me. I must run my race."

He knelt down and waved them over.

The gathering collected around him and placed their hands on him.

Paul lifted up his face and prayed, "Blessed are You, Yahweh. May Your face shine upon those gathered here. Keep them from those who seek to harm them and tear them away from the flock. Give them wisdom and courage."

When he was done praying, they each embraced him. Lea's tears mingled with theirs. She didn't understand what Paul was trying to tell them, but that seemed to be the consensus among the group.

"I must do one last thing before I go," Paul said. "Would you come here, Timothy?"

Lea released him so he could obey.

Paul waved to the ground in front of him. "Kneel."

He did.

"Men, would you come and lay hands on our young Timothy."

The men stretched out their hands to cover him.

"We commit you, Timothy, to Yahweh and to all He has for you in Ephesus."

At the mention of her home town, Lea almost yelped. What was Paul doing?

"We ask Yahweh to bless you as you shepherd the flock. Remain strong in the faith you have been taught and do not be afraid to lead."

As the hands cleared, Timothy rose and embraced Paul. They wept together until they had no more tears.

"I must catch my ship before it leaves without me.

Lea walked toward him.

He held out his hands to her and pulled her in close. "Sweet Lea. I return your husband to you safe as promised."

She couldn't stop the question that ripped at her heart from coming forth. "What did you mean when you said we won't see your face again?"

He held her cheeks and put his forehead to hers. It was an easy feat since they were roughly the same height. "What awaits me only Yahweh knows, but He has warned me I have a difficult road ahead."

"Then don't go." Her warm tears fell fresh.

He opened his eyes so they were staring straight into hers. "I must."

She threw her arms around his neck and kissed both his cheeks. "I will pray for you every day."

"The greatest gift one can give."

"Lea," Timothy called her over. "This is

Doctor Luke."

The man standing beside her husband was handsome and humble. His eyes held the kindness one would hope for in a physician.

"It's a pleasure to meet you," she offered. "I've heard so many wonderful things about you."

"And I you. Timothy has been speaking about nothing but you since they picked me up in Phillpi."

She smiled, then a thought struck her. "I do hope all is well in your party."

Luke and Timothy exchanged a glance.

"Paul's eyesight is acting up again. I've agreed to join him as long as he needs me."

Lea held on to Timothy while they waved off Paul from the docks. When the boat left their view, Timothy accompanied the elders and Lea back to Ephesus.

After prying Timothy away from the welcome of his mother and grandmother, Lea begged him to share everything that had happened in the months of his absence.

He settled in at the table. "When we left Ephesus, we sailed for Greece. We stayed in Corinth for about three months."

"Corinth?" Lea wondered.

"It seemed Titus was successful and straightening out the flock there and Paul wanted to visit them. Of course, Paul received word from

Priscilla and Aquila about the church in Rome. So, he sent off a letter to them during our stay."

"How are they?" Lea wondered.

"As well as to be expected. It seems persecution is not as cooled as we had hoped there, but they are happy to be home."

"I'm glad they are well."

"After three months, Paul wanted to go to Syria, but he received word that some Jews were lying in wait for him there. So, he changed course and we headed through Macedonia to visit some of the other churches. He sent some of the others on to Troas while he and I went to Phillpi to pick up Luke. I knew Paul wanted to speak with the elders of Ephesus, but I didn't know what he was going to say."

She hugged him. "It makes my heart glad to have you home."

"I missed being with you as well, but we had so many incredible encounters. It really did me good to spend the time learning again."

She smiled.

"When we all came back together in Troas, we had a meeting and Paul spoke for hours. I think he was trying to get everything he ever learned in because we had plans to leave the next day. Well, the hour dragged on and the room got so hot because of all the oil lamps. One of the young men named Eutychus, was sitting on the window-sill and fell asleep. The boy fell from the third loft."

"Oh no!"

"When I rushed down there with another man, we found him dead."

"The poor thing. I'm sure Paul felt awful."

"He came down and laid on top of the man saying, 'Don't worry because he still has life in him.' And the boy woke up."

"Amazing!"

"It sure was. We took the young man back upstairs and he continued eating and talking as if nothing happened."

"Praise Yahweh that He restored the man his life."

"The next day we sailed to Assos, Mitylene, Chios, then on to Samos and Trogyllium. Finally, we made it to Miletus. Paul told us his plan to go to Jerusalem. Luke has continued to try to talk him out of it, but Paul is sure. He feels as strongly about this call as any other."

"What do you think will happen?"

"I don't know for sure. But over the last several months, it has become clear that the Jews seek his life. It's just a matter of time before they get their way."

Lea set to her promise of praying for Paul. She had heard so many stories of him escaping death. She hoped Yahweh would once again spare him from the snares others tried to set for him.

Chapter Sixteen

"For thou shalt be his witness unto all men of what thou hast seen and heard." -Acts 22:15

A.D. 60

The fresh sea breeze of the Cayster River lifted Lea's heart. A settled life in Ephesus had done much to ease the ache for her dear ones scattered abroad. Though she stole away at least a few moments every day to come down to the bay to pray and hang on to a thin strand of hope that one of the ships coming into port would bring a familiar face.

Timothy had grown into his role as shepherd to their growing flock of Way followers. Joy filled her as her other two sisters came to the Way under his teaching. Each of the three of them had opened their homes to the spreading church. Her mother attended a few meetings, but made no public decision. Her father had continued in his comfortable role as Rabbi with no crack in his husk that she could see. Three of her nephews had also expressed desires to follow Jesus. The youngest niece enjoyed the stories, but was still not yet convinced of their devotion. Lea held out hope that Yahweh would draw her little heart to Himself too.

From experience, Lea knew no church was without its problems. When mixed backgrounds gather and pride prevails, it's only a matter of time before disagreements break out. Timothy had his hands full most weeks merely trying to correct his feuding flock. He made rounds speaking throughout the many house churches reminding them of the words of Jesus and the lessons of Paul.

Lea had grown more comfortable in her role of service beside her husband. With each family that came to the Way, the women seemed to need extra private reassurance. She spent much of her days traveling from house to house speaking words of encouragement and praying with overwhelmed mothers and hopeless housewives.

A ship unloaded nearby and she tilted her head at a man who disembarked with the rest of the passengers. "Luke?"

The doctor lifted his head and looked toward the sound of her voice. "Lea!" He waved.

She rushed toward him and greeted him with a simple kiss on the cheek. "It's good to see you."

He looked down and shook his head. "I'm afraid it's not for good I am here."

Her heart squeezed. "Come with me. I'll take

you to Timothy."

Once they had collected Luke's personal effects from the ship, Lea led him to their rented house.

Timothy greeted his friend and introduced him to his mother and grandmother while Lea prepared a plate of snacks and poured a fresh cup of water.

Luke sat and gave thanks to Yahweh before speaking, "I only wish this was a joyous visit. We've all missed you, brother Timothy."

"We are ready to hear whatever message you carry."

"When we left Ephesus, we made several stops on our journey to Jerusalem. One of which was Tyre. We found disciples of the Way there who were a great comfort to us. They kept telling us the Spirit was trying to stop Paul from going to Jerusalem. We stayed there for about a week before moving on to Caesarea, where we stayed with Philip. A prophet by the name of Agabus came from Judea to deliver a message to Paul."

"What was the message?"

"He took Paul's belt and bound his own hands and feet and told Paul that the Jews in Jerusalem would bind him as such and deliver him into the hands of the Gentiles."

"Poor Paul," Lea lamented.

"We begged him not to go. I begged him…"

Lasting Legacy

Luke looked up and Lea could see tears forming in his eyes.

Timothy put his hand on Luke's shoulder. "What happened?"

"Paul asked us why we were trying to break his heart and that he was ready to not only be imprisoned again, but also to die for the name of the Lord Jesus."

"No." Lea covered her mouth.

"What could we do?" He spread his hands over the table. "We had to let him go. So, we went on to Jerusalem. There we stayed with some disciples and Paul made a visit with James to tell him about all the work that had been done among the Gentiles."

"How did they take the news?" Timothy wondered.

"They rejoiced with us, but they suggested that Paul take a vow to prove to the Jews that he was not trying to turn Jews into Gentiles by telling them they couldn't follow their traditions any longer."

"Did he?" Lea asked.

"For seven days he fulfilled his vow. After he was done, he shaved his head and went to the Temple to show himself to the priest and offer sacrifices for himself and for the other four men. But there were Jews there who stirred the assembly when they saw Paul."

"What was their accusation?" Timothy asked.

"They said Paul had brought a Gentile into the inner court of the Temple."

"Who?"

"Trophimus."

"Our Trophimus?"

"The same. It seems they saw Paul with him in the city earlier and assumed he had brought him into the Temple. Which he didn't."

"Did they have any witnesses?"

"They provided themselves as witnesses. They got the crowd stirred up to the point they seized Paul and hauled him out of the Temple. They beat him until he was almost dead."

"Oh no." Lea covered her face.

"But the Romans stopped them."

"Praise Yahweh."

"A tribune by the name of Claudius Lysias arrested Paul and ordered he be bound with two chains."

"Just like in Agabus prophecy?"

"Exactly. The crowd was so confused about what had happened Lysias couldn't straighten things out and ordered Paul to be taken to the barracks. They had to carry Paul because the crowd was growing so violent. When they made it to the steps, Paul asked if he could speak. Once given permission, Paul gave his testimony right there in front of all those people."

"He takes any opportunity," Timothy agreed.

"It only further angered the crowd as they revolted so much that Lysias ordered Paul to be flogged."

Visions of a broken and bleeding back nearly sent Lea running from the room.

"The centurions had him on the table ready to beat him until Paul reminded them he was a Roman citizen and had not been officially condemned."

"Did they free him then?"

"No. They didn't flog him, but they kept him in jail for the night. The next day, Lysias put together a meeting with the chief priests and Paul to straighten out the issue. It didn't go as hoped."

"How bad?" Timothy asked.

"Ananias commanded the others to strike Paul in the mouth when he tried to defend himself. They exchanged words, but when Paul realized they were a mixed group of Pharisees and Sadducees, he asked them if he was on trial for believing in the resurrection of the dead."

"Oh no," Timothy dreaded.

"That's right. The simple question caused the entire assembly to divide and clamor against each other. Lysias had Paul removed fearing that they might rip him in two."

"I'm starting to appreciate this Claudius Lysias a great deal," Lea added.

"Paul later told us about a visit from Yahweh that night who stood beside him and told him not to be afraid and that he would testify in Rome."

"Rome?"

"That's what Yahweh said. Little did we know that about forty men plotted to kill Paul. They convinced the high priests to have Paul called before them so they could judge his case, but they were really going to take the opportunity to kill Paul."

"Paul!" Lea wept.

"Thankfully, Paul's nephew heard about the murderous plot and informed Paul. The information was then told to the centurion who informed Lysias. The tribune called two hundred soldiers with seventy horsemen and two hundred spearmen to escort Paul that night to Governor Felix along with a letter explaining everything that had happened."

"At least Paul made it out safely."

"They arrived and waited for his accusers to come down. Which they did. Paul was then given an opportunity to present his case. Which he did."

"What did Felix say?"

"He wanted to wait for Claudius Lysias to come as well. We were able to minister to Paul while he waited, but Felix called him again and this time he let his wife sit in on the hearing. When Paul spoke about self-control and the coming judgment, Felix didn't want to hear anymore and sent him back. We think he was waiting for Paul to bribe him because he had many conversations with Paul."

"Paul would never do such a thing."

"I know. This went on for two years until Porcius Festus took over as governor."

"Two years?" Timothy asked. "Paul has been rotting in jail for two years and this is the first we receive word?"

"He continued to have faith he would be released any day. When Festus came into power, the Jews attempted their plot again. But Festus wouldn't agree. Instead, he called them to meet him at Caesarea so that he could judge the matter."

"How did that hearing go?"

"The Jews weren't able to prove their case, so Festus asked Paul if he wanted to be tried in Jerusalem."

"I'm afraid to hear what Paul answered."

"I was afraid standing there. He told him he was appropriately standing before Caesar's tribunal though he had done nothing worthy of death. He reminded Fetus that if the Jews couldn't prove their case, then he had no right to hand him over to them and then he…"

"He what?"

"He appealed to Caesar."

"He didn't."

"He did. With no other choice, Festus agreed to send him to Caesar. Before that could happen, King Agrippa arrived at Caesarea and wanted to hear the case. Paul gave his testimony before the king."

"What did the king think of Paul's case?"

"He thought Paul was mad from all his knowledge."

"He sure comes across that way sometimes."

"The king and the governor didn't find any cause to put Paul to death, but since he had appealed to Caesar they couldn't release him either."

"So?"

"So on to Italy we go. I've come here on behalf of Paul. He has requested for you to join us on this voyage. A ship is waiting at Adramyttium."

Timothy looked at Lea.

"Another trip?"

"This one all the way to Rome. It will take months to get there."

"And back again."

He nodded.

"But Paul needs you."

"You need me and so do the churches."

"Yahweh will sustain us until your return."

He looked to Luke. "We must leave right away."

Lea whispered prayers for all of them. She knew it would be no easy task to send off her husband again, but if his presence meant peace to Paul, she would gladly deliver him herself.

"One request?" she urged.

"Anything, Wife."

"Give Priscilla and Aquila a hug from me. I miss them terribly."

Chapter Seventeen

"And Paul dwelt two whole years in his own hired house, and received all that came in unto him, Preaching the kingdom of God, and teaching those things which concern the Lord Jesus Christ, with all confidence, no man forbidding him." -Acts 28:30-31

A.D. 61

A letter from Timothy came over a year after his departure. Lea saved it to read at the next Way follower meeting. Though it was incredibly tempting to peer at a portion every now and then.

" 'Greetings,' " she read aloud, " 'from those of us in Rome. The day I left, we embarked on a ship from Adramyttium with Paul. A centurion named Julius allowed us to minister to Paul while we traveled. When we made it to Myra, the centurion found a ship of Alexandria and put us on board. The winds were contrary to us until we made it to Fair Havens. It took longer for us to make it there due to the rough seas and weather. Paul advised them to let us winter there because it was too dangerous to continue. They didn't pay attention to him because they didn't like the port and decided to chance the journey to Phoenix.

" 'We had to weigh anchor and sail along Crete because of the south winds. Then a northeaster struck down on us and we could not face the wind any longer. We desperately tried to secure the ship, but we were so violently driven by the storm that we had to dump cargo. For fourteen days, we didn't see the sun or stars because of the great storm over us. All hope of being saved was abandoned.' "

Lea's hands shook the parchment. She had to take a breath to steady herself before she continued, " 'Paul stood among them and reminded them that they should have listened to him. He encouraged them that no one would lose their life, but the ship would be destroyed. An angel of Yahweh had made the promise to him the previous night.

" 'When we came too close to land, the sailors feared the ship would run aground. They let down the anchors and prayed for day. They tried to let down small boats in which to escape, but Paul told them that only the people who stayed on the ship would survive. The soldiers cut the ropes holding the boats so no one could leave.

" 'We eventually struck the reef and ran aground. When the ship began to break, the soldiers planned to kill all the prisoners on board so they wouldn't escape. They didn't want to kill Paul, so the centurions stopped them. Julius prepared a plan to get everyone to shore by using planks for those who couldn't swim.

" 'The island we made it to was Malta. The people were very welcoming and built a fire for us. As Paul gathered sticks for the fire, a viper struck his hand. The people saw the snake hanging from his hand and believed he was a murderer receiving his punishment. Paul simply shook off the creature and went about his collecting.' "

Lea's heart raced a little faster.

" 'The people watched Paul waiting for him to die from the venom, but he didn't. This made them believe Paul was a god. The chief of the island, a man named Publius, allowed us to lodge at his home for three days.

" 'When his father became ill, Paul visited him and prayed over him. Thanks be to Yahweh; the man was healed. Word spread about the healing and the rest of the people on the island brought their sick to Paul for him to pray for them. Yahweh cured all of them.

" 'After three months there, we found a ship that had wintered there and were able to secure passage to Rome. When we boarded the ship, the people of the island honored us by bringing many supplies to us so that we had more than we needed for our journey.

" 'Many brothers awaited us at Rome. Paul called the Jews together to explain his case. They expressed their concern for him and revealed they had received no letter from the Jews in Judea about Paul. For an entire day, Paul spoke to them about the kingdom of Yahweh and trying to convince them about Jesus.

" 'Some were convinced, but others didn't believe. The Romans are allowing Paul to live in a rented house with his guard. Anyone is free to come and hear about Jesus without hindrance. Though we don't know when Paul will be brought before Caesar, we praise Yahweh that Paul is free enough to continue teaching. Many have come to the Way. Pray for us as we pray for you.' "

Lea rolled up the letter and set it down. "Let us pray together for those in Rome and for a speedy trial for Paul."

The church huddled together in the rented house lifting their requests in one accord to the One who could be with them and those miles away at the same time.

Another year kept Lea in constant prayer for her far-away husband. She visited with as many women as she could if for nothing else than to keep her thoughts occupied. The elders kept their house churches in order as much as they could, but with the lack of leadership it became challenging to keep all the fractured people in line. Lea spent more and more time waiting at the bay for a ship carrying her loved ones home or at least a word about them. No other letter had come.

With a heavy heart, she returned home to spend the heat of the day with her in-laws in the rented house. The other two women prepared a simple meal and encouraged her as best they could.

When a familiar face finally came knocking on her door, Lea couldn't contain her joy.

"Oh, Paul!" She embraced the older man.

He held her for a long time before finally holding her at arm's length. "It is so good to see you, young one."

"Luke! Tychicus!" She kissed the cheeks of the other men with him. "But where is Timothy?"

They entered and sat at the table.

"Your husband will be along shortly," Paul explained. "I sent him to Philippi to encourage the church there."

"How did you gain your freedom?"

"I believe I have our dear Luke here to thank." He put a hand on the other man's shoulder. "He wrote a letter to his friend, Theophilus, who was able to give it as testimony before the court."

"And the rest of the group?"

"Most of the others have returned to their own homes to continue spreading the message. We did stop in Crete to preach and I left Titus there to minister to the small church."

In less than two weeks, Lea was reunited with her Timothy. Only a few short days later, Paul boarded a ship to Macedonia. With his newly found freedom, he wanted to use any time given to teach about the Way.

Lea clung to Timothy praying that their time of separation was finally over. She didn't think she could ever let him board another ship even if Jesus came asking Himself.

Chapter Eighteen

"As I besought thee to abide still at Ephesus, when I went into Macedonia, that thou mightest charge some that they teach no other doctrine,"
-1 Timothy 1:3

A.D. 65

Lea sang along with their group of Way followers, "If we have died with Him, we will also live with Him. If we endure, we will also reign with Him. If we deny Him, He also will deny us. If we are faithless, He remains faithful, for He cannot deny Himself."

Timothy stood and signaled the group to join him in their final blessing, "Yahweh was manifested in the flesh, vindicated by the Spirit, seen by angels, proclaimed among the nations, believed on in the world, and taken up into glory."

As the crowd dispersed, Lea caught a face she hadn't seen in years. "Priscilla?"

The older woman stood off to the side with her husband. She wore a bright smile that lit up her eyes. "Greetings."

The two embraced and squealed as if they had both traveled back to their youth.

"What are you doing here?" Lea asked.

"It seems home was not as welcoming as we would have liked."

Aquila took his turn to greet Lea. "It wasn't home that had a problem with us. It was that new Emperor."

"Aquila. Priscilla." Timothy found the group. "We didn't receive word of your visit."

"That's because we didn't send any," Aquila explained. "My wife thought a surprise visit would be more appropriate."

Priscilla took Lea's hands in hers. "Were you surprised?"

"Pleasantly. I have prayed for you often."

"Will you two do us the honor of joining us for a meal?" Timothy asked.

"I thought you'd never offer." Aquila nudged the young man. "I want to hear all about this growing flock of yours."

Timothy's face darkened. "Of course."

Lea spoke up, "Priscilla, will you help me in the kitchen?"

The two women excused themselves to make preparations.

"What's going on?" Priscilla whispered as soon as they were far enough away from the men.

"Timothy has been having trouble with some

of the followers. They are struggling with staying committed to the teachings. Many of them want to include the former things they are familiar with and add them to what he tries to teach them. Some days he says he feels as if he is beating the ocean back with a stick."

"I see." She went to work filling the serving platters with fresh fruit. "It's not always as easy as Paul makes it seem."

"Speaking of Paul. Have you spoken with him lately?"

"We met up with him in Macedonia on our way here. Aquila has a letter for Timothy."

"I'm sure he will be most encouraged by a word from his mentor."

"Where are Timothy's mother and grandmother? I didn't see them at the meeting."

Her eyes watered. "I'm afraid we lost both of them last year."

"I'm sorry to hear that. They were such sweet women."

"They were a great comfort to me. But I do not weep. They both held such joy for wanting to be in the presence of their Savior. Their one small drip of concern was that they weren't sure if they would see their Hector there."

"He never came to the Way?"

"Not publicly. Each held to a few conversations they were able to have with him and a handful of meetings he attended. We never know the true condition of another's soul."

They placed the platters on the table and joined the men.

"Priscilla tells me they just came from seeing Paul," Lea offered.

"Oh?" Timothy perked up.

"Yes." Aquila patted his tunic. "I've got a letter here for you." He revealed a scroll and passed it to Timothy.

"I'll be sure to read it later." He set the parchment off to the side. "Is Paul still in Macedonia?"

"I'm afraid he was preparing to head to Rome."

"Rome?" Lea choked on a sip of water. "Didn't you just leave there?"

Aquila reached over and patted his wife's hand. "Under much protest, yes."

"Will you tell us what happened?" Timothy wondered.

"It all started with a fire last year."

"It raged for nine days," Priscilla added.

"When the flames were finally subdued, ten of the fourteen regions were left in ruins." Aquila folded his arms and leaned on his forearms. "Emperor Nero was quick to provide shelter, but it wasn't long after that he announced he was going to confiscate one hundred and twenty-five acres of private land to build himself a new palace with a lavish garden."

"Then the rumors started," Priscilla said. "It seemed the one who benefited from the fire was probably the one who started it."

"You think Nero burned Rome for his own gain?" Lea asked.

"We're not sure," Aquila answered. "But the timing added up and people were ready to place blame. Nero wasn't prepared to take the fall, so he decided to deflect the attention on something else."

"You mean *someone* else," Priscilla corrected.

"Who?" Lea wondered.

"Us." Aquila let the idea sink in. "Nero dreamed of more outlandish methods to persecute Way followers. He dressed some in animal skins and allowed them to be torn to pieces by wild dogs. Others he crucified. And worse yet…"

Priscilla rubbed his back. "The worse one of all was that he would light them on fire while they still drew breath and used them as lamps to light up his gardens." Tears slid down her cheeks.

"How awful." Lea didn't hold back her own sorrow.

"We couldn't stay there," Aquila spoke through quivering lips. "It was becoming too dangerous."

"We knew where Paul was and so we stopped there to catch up with him."

"When we shared with him everything we'd seen, he was determined to go strengthen the church at Rome."

"He can't," Lea demanded.

"He might not be able to," Priscilla agreed. "The sailing season to Italy is almost over."

"Paul will find a way," Timothy said. "He might not ask others to go with him this time, but he has nothing tying him down. He'll go."

As the men spoke in hushed tones, Priscilla joined Lea in the kitchen to clean up.

"How has Yahweh treated you?"

Lea smiled. "Despite our church struggles, we continue to grow."

"It's always hard."

"It's even more difficult for Timothy. The Jews who join come from a culture where respect is earned in years. It's difficult for them to respect a younger leader. But many have come to the Way including all of my own sisters."

"Praise Yahweh."

"He is truly deserving of such praise."

"And what of you and Timothy?"

Lea hesitated.

"Oh." The older woman needed no words to understand the open wound she had revealed. "I'm sorry."

"We've been trying to grow our family ever since Timothy returned from his last mission trip." She shrugged. "Yahweh simply hasn't seen fit to grant our request." A single tear slipped out.

"My dear." She wrapped a warm arm around her and held her tight. "I know the hurt you feel."

"You and Aquila?"

She nodded. "It's not easy, but we gave that hurt over to Yahweh a long time ago. Some days it still pounds fresh in this old heart. My arms ache and my soul feels fractured as if something is missing."

"That's exactly what it feels like."

"But do you want to know what helped me the most?"

Lea wiped her face and nodded.

"Paul told me once that I was already a mother, even if I never gave birth to my own child."

"What does that mean?"

"He was trying to say that all the women I've been able to pour into are like my spiritual children. Just like Timothy and many of the others are like Paul's sons. I have had the privilege of teaching so many wonderful women. The most beloved of all being you." She squeezed her again.

Lea beamed. "I always thought of you as another mother."

"Being a spiritual mother has never replaced my longing to be a physical mother, but it has done my soul well. To see each woman come to faith in Jesus and take those steps on the path of obedience is something I wouldn't trade for the whole world.

"Still, if I got pregnant tomorrow, I'd be the happiest woman alive. For, you see, one joy doesn't have to replace another. I can rejoice in being a spiritual mother and still have a desire to hold my own baby. The trick is not to allow the sorrow of one to taint the joy of the other. To not allow the grief to consume you to the point you can't do the things Yahweh has called you to do. That doesn't mean to hide it away. Merely keep it in light of all Yahweh has blessed you with. It still doesn't mean we stop hurting."

"I think I understand."

"I will pray that Yahweh opens your womb."

"You can count on my prayers for you as well."

"I'm nearing the last years of that possibility."

"That's what Sarah thought too." Lea winked.

Chapter Nineteen

"Thou therefore endure hardness, as a good soldier of Jesus Christ." -2 Timothy 2:3

A.D. 68

Lea and Priscilla prepared the mid-day meal when a knock at the door interrupted them.

"I'll see who it is." Lea wiped her hand on a rag and made her way to the door.

When she opened it, she was greeted with the face of an old friend. "Tychicus!"

"Greetings." He bowed. "May I come in?"

"Of course." She waved him inside. "It is so good to see you. Are you well?"

"I am, but I'm afraid the news I carry is not at all well."

Lea put her hands to her chest. "Paul?"

He nodded.

"Let me get Timothy." She rushed to the back of the house where they had set up a place for Timothy to study in private. "Tychicus is here to see you."

A brief moment of joy was overshadowed by

concern. He wasted no time in following her to the main area where their friend waited.

The men greeted each other warmly.

Timothy squeezed Tychicus' arm. "Lea tells me you have news. Please speak on."

"I'm afraid our companion Paul has found himself in another set of chains."

The vision of Paul shackled forced Lea to sink to a nearby stool.

Timothy motioned for their guest to sit at the table. "It's not the first time." He rubbed the back of his neck.

"It's Rome."

"Not the first time in Rome either." Timothy joined him at the table.

Tychicus looked down. "I'm afraid it's different this time. He sits in the Mamertine dungeon." He slowly drew out a scroll from his bag. "This is for you."

Timothy took the outstretched parchment. "For me or the churches?"

"Both."

He unrolled it. "Have you read it?"

"On my word as a messenger, no. But Luke scribed it. He mentioned its weight."

Timothy's eyes darted quickly over the letter.

"He's begging for you."

Timothy read and re-read portions. "It sounds like a…"

"Like a last will and testament. That's what Luke said."

"He doesn't have hope of release?"

"Not this time."

"No hope?" Lea whimpered.

Tychicus turned to look at her. "A different kind of hope."

Timothy read part of the letter out loud, " 'For I am already being poured out as a drink offering, and the time of my departure has come. I have fought the good fight. I have finished the race. I have kept the faith.

" 'Henceforth there is laid up for me the crown of righteousness, which the Lord, the righteous judge, will award to me on that day, and not only to me but also to all who have loved His appearing.' "

"He thinks Yahweh is calling him to die?" Lea asked.

"He's convinced of it," Tychicus answered.

"But he's gotten out of imprisonment before."

"With Yahweh's help each time." He folded his hands on the table. "He believes this will be his last sentence."

Timothy laid the scroll on the table. "What led to this?"

"When Paul heard about what was happening to the Way followers in Rome, he had to move fast. The sailing season to Italy was getting ready to close."

"He mentions something about Trophimus being ill."

He nodded. "When Paul left Ephesus, he intended to go to Macedonia but traveled to Miletus first."

"Why?"

"To retrieve me. Unfortunately, Trophimus fell ill there that no amount of praying would heal. Paul had no choice but to leave him there and continue on without him."

"Is he still there?"

"I've received word that he is still there and recovering from his illness. I will visit him as soon as I am able."

"I wish I would have heard sooner that he was nearby. We would have tended to him."

"I had wished we had time to stop in Ephesus. It would have been nice to visit and we could have shared the news about our brother. But we had to board a ship quickly that was bound toward Macedonia. It did make a short stop at Troas. We stayed with Carpus until the ship was ready to leave."

"We need to stop there before heading to Rome." Timothy searched the scroll. "It seems Paul left some personal effects there."

"The ship was full of passengers. He wanted to lighten our load. We made it to Macedonia and visited several of the churches, including Corinth."

Timothy held his head. "He went back to Corinth?"

"Paul had a deep longing to visit with them. We even stayed with Erastus."

"Is he well?" Lea wondered.

"Yes. Paul asked him to journey on with us, but he declined. With the season change bearing down on us, Paul decided to winter at Nicopolis so we could be ready to take the first ship to Rome as soon as possible. The time was too long for Demas and he decided to turn back and return to Thessalonica. Paul sent Crescens to Galatia and Titus to Dalmatia."

"I thought Titus was in Crete," Timothy said.

"He was, but Paul sent Artemas to relieve him. Titus joined us in Nicopolis, but Paul wanted to send him on to Dalmatia. It was soon after our arrival there that Paul was arrested and put on a ship to Rome."

"I guess that's one way to reach his destination," Priscilla joked.

The others didn't laugh.

"A trip of over a thousand miles is going to take months to complete," Timothy reasoned.

"Then we shall leave at once," Lea added.

"We?"

"You have left me here enough times. I will not

budge on this decision. I am going with you to Rome. If Paul believes these truly are his last days among us, then I want to see his face one more time."

"It's far too dangerous to bring you there."

"There is no safe place anymore. I'd rather stand with you than cower here."

Priscilla stepped forward. "Aquila and I will join you."

"I can't ask you to do that." Timothy shook his head.

"Rome is our home. We know it better than anywhere. We can be a help to you there."

"The other problem is the churches. I can't ask them to do without me again."

"That's why Paul sent me."

They all turned to Tychicus.

"I'm not just a messenger. I'm here as your replacement for however long it takes for your return."

"It seems all is settled." Priscilla grabbed her headwrap. "I'll go inform Aquila and help him close up the booth."

Timothy rose. "I need to go find John Mark. He'll need time to prepare for the journey."

Before sunset the next day, the group boarded a ship to Troas.

When they landed, they found the home of Carpus.

The older man welcomed them. "I'm sorry to hear of Paul's imprisonment, but I have to say I'm not surprised."

"We are here to collect some of his belongings."

Carpus scratched his bearded chin. "I do remember him leaving some things behind. Let me see if I can locate them."

He searched his home and retrieved Paul's cloak, scrolls, and parchments. He turned them over to Timothy. "I believe that's all of it."

"Thank you."

"Would your group like to stay the night?"

"I'm afraid we can't." Timothy looked to the others. "We have a long journey ahead of us."

"I understand. May Yahweh go with you."

They purchased passage on a ship headed for Macedonia.

Lea stood on the bow of the boat letting the sea air refresh her. She never thought she'd ever stand on the wooden planks of another ship again. The sea had called to her from her youth and the frustrating time abroad had sealed her decision to stay in Ephesus. Somehow, the fresh taste of saltwater stirred the longing in her heart to go. She wasn't sure what awaited any of them in Rome, but there was something no one could deny. The same Jesus she met in Ephesus would be with them in Rome. Of that fact, she was certain.

"We are traveling farther than you've ever been." Timothy came up behind her and rubbed her shoulders. "Danger may be lurking for us."

She leaned into his broad chest. "Danger can seek us anywhere, even at home. I want to see him."

"As do I. But I can't shake this feeling that I should have left all of you in Ephesus."

"You didn't drag any of us against our wills. We all came willingly to see Paul."

"It doesn't ease my fear."

"Let Yahweh do that."

He nodded and closed his eyes.

Lea could make out parts of his whispered prayer. She too joined his pleas.

They docked in Nicopolis long enough to confirm the details of Paul's arrest and find a ship sailing for Rome.

After four months and several changes of ships, their last boat finally traveled up the Tiber River to the newly dedicated port of Ostia.

Lea could hardly believe her eyes. The grand city of Rome she had heard of from the lips of friends now stood stretched out before her. Her heart pounded. She wanted to be raptured by all Rome had to offer, but the excitement of a new city was quickly turned to sorrow when she remembered the goal of their long journey. Paul sat in a dungeon waiting to see Timothy one last time before he left this world. She was going to do her best to give him that gift and add a few measures of her own encouragement.

Chapter Twenty

"And the Lord shall deliver me from every evil work, and will preserve me unto his heavenly kingdom: to whom be glory for ever and ever. Amen." -2 Timothy 4:18

Rome

Lea watched the centurion's red cloak sway behind him as they followed him deeper into the prison. A set of stairs led them down into an empty cell.

"Where is Paul?" Timothy asked the guard.

He pointed to a hole in the ground that was covered by a small wooden door.

Timothy pulled on the handle and lifted the door away. He peered down into the darkness. "Paul?"

"Timothy, my son, is that you?" a voice echoed up through the hole.

"It is. I have John Mark with me too." He waved them over. "Priscilla and Aquila have accompanied me along with Lea."

The group took turns gazing into the opening.

Lea looked last. The only light in the dungeon came from the hole she had to partially block in order to see. After a few moments of her eyes adjusting, she could see Paul standing underneath with chains on his hands and feet.

"Greetings, young one," he shouted up. "It is good to see your face."

She smiled as tears rushed down her cheeks. "I've missed seeing yours too."

The group crowded around the hole.

"Are you well?" Timothy asked.

"No one can take Christ away from me so they can't take my joy."

"I have the things you requested." He dropped the items into the opening.

Lea heard each one fall.

"Thank you, Son. These will bring me much comfort."

They spoke as long as they could before the guards told them it was time to leave.

"Lea?" Paul called up to her.

She moved to look down.

"It does my heart well to see you beside Timothy."

"I do my best."

"I'm sure you've done a great deal more than that."

"I'm not so sure."

"I told you many years ago, young one, that

Jesus chooses unique vessels to do His work. You are a unique vessel, Lea. He will continue to do His work through you if you let Him."

She nodded. "We came to comfort you, yet you have comforted us."

"Yahweh remains with you. Remain in Him."

Lea blew a kiss down to him and stood.

Once outside the prison, silence covered the group.

"I suppose we should check on our home," Aquila offered.

They made their way to their house that stood quiet and abandoned.

Priscilla set to work dusting, but Aquila moved to grab her arm. "It can wait. I think we should all get a good night's sleep."

She nodded and put down her rag.

They showed Timothy and Lea a spare room upstairs while the rest of the group settled in among the house.

Try as she might, Lea couldn't sleep. She laid awake staring at the ceiling. She imagined herself in the deep dungeon where Paul sat. She wondered if he was asleep at that very moment or singing a hymn as he did with Silas the night the angel freed them. Tears rolled down her face. There would be no midnight rescue tonight. It seemed Paul would finally face the wrath of Rome.

The next day, Lea mindlessly fiddled around

Priscilla's kitchen. Her hands already knew what to do which freed her mind to wander back to Paul and his predicament. She stretched the limits of her imagination as they waited for word from Timothy and John Mark who had gone to see Paul as soon as the sun rose.

She was so lost in her own thoughts that she didn't hear the men come in until Priscilla addressed them.

"Have you any news?" the older woman asked.

"Paul has given testimony before Nero Caesar. He has had his day in court and he has been found guilty. Nero has sentenced him to be beheaded," Timothy announced.

"What?" Lea clutched herself.

"It is actually a gift."

"A gift?" She threw up her hands. "Why do you say such a thing?"

"Better than days of suffering on a cross or hours of torture being fed to the lions. Due to his Roman citizenship, they have agreed to a beheading. It's actually the most honorable and merciful way to die according to the Romans."

"This is madness. They released him before."

"We've exhausted all our resources. I'm afraid there is nothing more that can be done."

John Mark cleared his throat. "I've spoken with Paul. I do not wish to be present for his death. I'm boarding a ship to Alexandria today. I need to continue to spread the message of the Way."

Lea saw the sadness in his eyes. She imagined he had seen enough mentors die to last him a lifetime. "Of course. We shall pray for smooth seas."

"They would be welcomed."

Lea kissed his cheek. "It was good to work alongside you. I'm glad you got a chance to reconcile with Paul."

"I will send word upon my arrival," he promised over his shoulder as he left.

"They are preparing for the execution now," Timothy explained. "I'm heading back."

Lea lifted her headcloth and adjusted it. "I'm going too."

"No."

She looked up at him.

His gaze was steely and set. "I can't let you see that."

She stared right back at him.

"That image can't be removed once it has entered your mind."

"My mind is creative enough to come up with its own renditions. I want to be there for him."

"Please, Lea. Stay here."

"Is that an order?"

"It's a strong suggestion, but I can make it one if I need to."

"Then you'll just have to forgive my

disobedience."

"We'll all be there," Priscilla agreed. "None of us can be swayed."

When the sun was at it's highest, they joined the crowd gathered around Paul. He was chained to several guards.

A guard read off his formal charges, "Paul of Tarsus. By order of Nero, you have been found guilty of treason, heresy, and sacrilege against the law, against the temple, and against Caesar. For your crimes, you are to be beheaded."

The guards moved him forward and forced him to kneel.

Paul looked up toward the sky.

A soldier drew his sword, lifted it, and struck Paul's neck.

Lea closed her eyes, but it was too late. The image of Paul's head landing on the street was burned into her mind.

Timothy wrapped his arms around her.

When Lea opened her eyes again, a flood of red capes headed their direction.

"Timothy of Ephesus?" one of the Roman soldiers asked.

"What's this about?"

"For conspiracy with Paul of Tarsus, you are to be bound."

Two of the soldiers took each of Timothy's arms.

Lea pulled his tunic. "You can't take him!"

Another guard ripped Lea away and tossed her down.

Priscilla appeared by her side. "Don't fight them. They'll take you in too."

"Get her back to the house," Aquila ordered. "I'm going to go collect Paul's things and then I'll meet you there."

Lea leaned on Priscilla all the way to her house.

Priscilla sat her down and fixed her a snack. "Eat," she ordered. "You need your strength."

"Can they do that?" She didn't look up from her bowl. "Can they just take him like that?"

"It's Rome. They are in charge here."

A knock at the door a few hours later stirred the group.

"I'll get it," Aquila offered.

A lovely woman entered.

"Lucina." Priscilla greeted her. "I wasn't expecting you."

"I received word about Paul and have come to do whatever I can."

"That's very kind of you."

"I have a place you can bury him."

She nodded. "I'll make arrangements to have

the body released to you."

Lea came close.

"Lucina, this is Lea from Ephesus. She is Timothy's wife."

"Oh, my dear. I was so sorry to hear of your husband's imprisonment."

She bowed her head.

"Know that our church is praying for you."

"Speaking of church," Pricilla added. "Aquila and I are starting one again in our home. Could you help spread the word?"

"It would be a pleasure. Meeting in large groups is starting to draw unwanted attention."

Aquila entered. "Lucina." He greeted her. "I was hoping we would meet you here."

"My hope would have been under calmer circumstances, but it's good to see you none the less."

"I see you've met our Lea."

"We were just getting acquainted." She smiled. "Your wife tells me you're planning on starting another house church."

"Of course."

"The others will be happy to hear it. When can you begin meeting?"

"As soon as possible."

"Our group is gathering tomorrow. Why don't you join us?"

"We'd be honored."

The following day, Lea followed Aquila and Priscilla to Lucina's home.

With a heavy heart, she spoke of Timothy's imprisonment and thanked the group for their prayers. The time together did much to revive her soul and strength.

Word spread through Rome and it didn't take long before Aquila and Priscilla's home became a thriving church once more. Lea served where she could make her hands useful. She spent her precious free time visiting Timothy and encouraging him.

"It sounds wonderful," Timothy praised her.

"We are meeting later today."

"I will pray Aquila's words bring many to the Way."

Lea smiled at him through the bars. "I must go now."

Timothy lifted a chained hand to brush her cheek. "I will await your next visit."

During the mid-day break, the house filled with bodies.

Lea wondered if the walls could contain them all.

"Perhaps we should seek out other buildings," Priscilla offered. "How is Timothy?"

"In good spirits."

"I'm sure that has much to do with your visits."

"I'm just glad his Ima and Safta Lois are not

alive to see him in chains."

"They would have been proud to see him following Yahweh."

Lea looked around the room. So many had come to hear the words of life. She thanked Yahweh that long ago her husband had heard the message and committed his path to the steps Yahweh ordered.

As Aquila moved to the front of the room, a knock came at the door.

A nearby person opened it.

In poured dozens of Roman soldiers, causing the crowd to panic and scatter.

Priscilla grabbed Lea. "Take as many as you can out the back. Run to Lucina's. She'll protect you."

"What about you?" Lea protested.

"Do as I say." She pushed her toward the back.

Lea pressed her way through the crowd urging others to follow.

She ran as fast as her feet would carry her to Lucina's home and called through the back door.

Lucina found her there weeping. "What has happened?"

"It's Priscilla. Romans raided the meeting and I don't know what has happened. She told me to run." Lea panted. "I didn't want to leave her there, but she ordered me away."

Lucina pulled her inside. "Go upstairs and

hide yourself. I'll seek word."

Lea rushed the stairs two at a time and found an empty room. She crawled under the bed and watched the door. The house was quiet for a long time.

At some point, she fell asleep and was roused when the front door creaked open. She held her breath waiting for the sandaled feet of a Roman guard to come in and drag her away.

"Lea?" the soft voice of Lucina called down the hallway.

She crawled out from under the bed and met her at the door. She wrapped the woman in an embrace. "I'm so glad it's you."

"I have word. Priscilla and Aquila, along with many of the others have been taken prisoner. The Romans found out about their house church."

Lea covered her mouth. "Oh no!"

"Don't worry." She held her cheek. "You're safe here. But I don't want you visiting the jail right now. Not until things settle down."

"But Timothy—"

"Will understand."

After weeks of hiding in Lucina's house, Lea received dreadful word from a messenger and demanded to see her husband.

"I don't think it's a good idea."

"But this is important. I need to tell them face to face."

Lucina tapped her jaw. "I think I might just have a way."

She lifted one of her dresses up to her. "We are about the same size."

Lea looked down at the garment.

"They will be looking for a Jewess. Perhaps they will overlook a Roman woman."

As the sun shone bright, Lea made her way toward the prison. She took a steadying breath and pretended to carry herself with confidence as Lucina had shown her. The guards barely gave her a second look as they opened the gate to let her in.

She made her way to the large cell where Aquila sat with Timothy.

"Lea?" Timothy asked.

"I have news."

"You need to leave immediately. It's not safe for our kind here."

"I will as soon as I deliver this message."

"Speak quickly then."

"It's John Mark."

At the mention of the name, both men perked up.

"He made it to Alexandria, but it seems his teaching caused quite a stir. The people there didn't like that he tried to lead others away from their gods. So, they placed…" She grabbed her throat and tried to speak past the lump rising up. "They tied a rope around his neck and pulled him through the streets until he was dead."

Timothy bowed his head.

"The poor boy," Aquila uttered.

Lea looked around. "Where's Pricilla?"

"They have taken her to another part of the jail."

"I must go see her." Lea tiptoed up the stairs. She heard Timothy's and Aquila's muffled pleas for her to return to them, but she didn't turn back.

"Priscilla," she whispered down the corridor.

A hand waved. "Here I am."

Lea rushed toward the cell.

Priscilla held onto the bars. "What are you doing here?"

"I came to see you."

"It's not safe for you here. If they believe you to be a Way follower, they won't hesitate to put you in a matching set of chains."

"Lucina gave me one of her dresses to blend in."

Priscilla looked further down.

"She even curled my hair."

"Well, now don't you look just like a true Roman woman."

"I had to come see all of you. To tell you…"

"What's happened?"

"It's John Mark. He was murdered in Alexandria."

"He is with the Lord now." Priscilla reached for her through the bars. "It does my soul well to see you. I hoped you were safe."

"I ran to Lucina. I told her about the raid. She wants you to know she is praying for all of you."

"We could sure use all the prayers we can get."

Lea couldn't halt her tears. "I can't believe they put you in here."

"Do not sorrow for me. I go to see my Lord." Tears streamed down her face. "He waits for me."

"I can't let you go."

"Oh, but you must. You know, I may not have carried you in my womb, but I've carried you in my heart since our first meeting. There are many more daughters out there waiting to be nurtured by a spiritual mother."

Lea shook her head. "I need you."

"You haven't needed me in a very long time." Priscilla wiped her face.

"That's not true."

"They need you, Lea."

She heard the sound of marching feet.

"Go quickly, dear one. Keep yourself safe. For Timothy's sake."

Lea squeezed her hand and then kissed it before rushing down the corridor. She rounded the corner and stopped. Curiosity overcame her and she peered back around the wall.

A group of guards stood in front of Priscilla's cell. One of them had Aquila by his chains.

"Priscilla of Rome?" the head guard asked.

"Yes."

"By order of Emperor Nero, you and your husband are to be beheaded for your crimes."

Lea covered a scream.

The guard unlocked the cell and hauled Priscilla out by her chain.

She met Lea's gaze and mouthed, "Run."

Lea didn't wait another second. She rushed toward the nearest door and ran all the way back to Lucina's.

"They are to be killed!" She pulled on Lucina. "Come quickly!"

The woman wasted no time in following Lea toward Capitol Hill.

In the open street, Lea watched as Aquila and Priscilla were read their formal charges.

The two stood next to each other as they had spent their entire lives.

Lea couldn't contain her sorrow. She wailed as loud as her voice would allow.

Aquila was pushed ahead toward the center where he knelt in front of a pedestal and laid his head down.

A guard stepped forward, drew his sword, and hit Aquila's neck with a clean slice.

"No!" Lea cried.

Another guard lifted the body away.

Priscilla was led to the same spot and knelt.

Lea dug her fingers into her scalp.

The guard lifted his bloody sword and hit his second mark with equal precision.

Lea turned into Lucina's open arms and wept aloud.

Lucina stroked her hair. "They can lie with Paul. I will make sure of it."

"I need to go see Timothy."

"I'll go with you. I'm not letting you out of my sight."

The two women stood in front of Timothy's cell and recounted what had happened.

"I should have never allowed them to come."

"This isn't your fault," Lea told him.

"But if I had made them stay in Ephesus…"

"They would have found a way to Rome."

He nodded.

"Don't worry about Lea." Lucina wrapped an arm around her. "She is going to stay with me until your release."

"I don't think—"

She held up her hand. "Until your release."

He nodded. "Until then."

The women sat in the stillness of the evening in Lucina's house, neither knowing what to say.

A quick rap on the door sent Lea into a panic.

Lucina placed a finger on her lips and pointed to the stairs.

Lea tiptoed away and made it to the top step when Lucina called her back.

"Lea, this is Zelia." She waved to the other woman. "She's a member of our church. Zelia, tell her what you told me."

"It's the Emperor."

Lea's breath caught in her throat.

"He had been tried in absentia and condemned to death as a public enemy. When he found out about this, he fell on his own sword."

"What does that mean?"

"Galba has been declared Emperor."

She wrapped her arms around herself as her breathing labored. "What does this mean for Timothy?"

"Only time will tell."

Lea's sorrow poured out in wails and cries. She begged Yahweh into the morning hours to secure her husband's release. There were no others to stand on his behalf. Only the Creator could bend the heart of the current occupant of the Roman throne.

Chapter Twenty-One

"Lord, they have killed thy prophets, and digged down thine altars; and I am left alone, and they seek my life." -Romans 11:3

A.D. 70

Lea folded the clothes she had spent the morning cleaning in the river. Lucina had lovingly offered her a room in her home, clothes to wear, and food to fill her stomach for almost two years. Though Lea thought of the rented house in Ephesus often. She had spoken with Onesiphorus on his last visit to Rome. He assured her the home was still being used for Way follower meetings and would be there when they returned.

If they returned, she wanted to correct him.

Lucina's house was often space for those seeking answers to their questions and weekly meetings for Way followers. Lucina's children were grown and living on their own. Her husband had been killed in one of the first waves of persecution by Nero. Despite everything, Lucina pressed on in obedience to Yahweh. Lea managed each day to keep enough strength to help where she could and visit Timothy in jail when Lucina deemed it safe. Those were few and far between. Each night she wept into her mattress for the safety of her husband and herself until they could leave Rome.

A knock at the door tore Lea back to the moment. She wiped her face and opened the door.

Timothy stood on the other side. He was dirty and the stench that rolled off him made her stomach turn. But she practically leapt into his arms.

"Timothy!" She kissed his filthy cheeks over and over again. Her tears mingled with his. "Praise Yahweh you are free!"

"I am." He held on tight to her and carried her inside.

She set her feet down. "How did it happen?"

His eyes darkened. "The change of Emperors caused a lot of confusion. Galba was murdered by Otho after only a year in power. He didn't make it three months when he chose to commit suicide rather than fight.

"Vitellius was proclaimed new Emperor, but when he realized his support was wavering, he prepared to abdicate in favor of Vespasian. When the soldiers heard of his decision, they decided to execute him and the next day Vespasian was declared Emperor by the Senate. His first order was to send his son Titus to lead an assault on the stronghold in Jerusalem. As Vespasian made changes to the guards, he set free some prisoners who had been left there under Nero. He decided that I had served enough time to learn my lesson. With the condition that I leave Rome."

"Whatever it takes." She hugged him tight. "I'm just glad you're free."

The door creaked behind them.

"Timothy?" Lucina entered. "You're free!"

He kissed her cheek. "I am."

"How did you know where to find us?"

"Aquila told me of your home while we sat in chains. He spoke very highly of you."

"I miss them."

"As do I." Timothy rubbed his writs. "It was so lonely without them there. But I was able to minister to several other prisoners."

"Paul would be proud," Lea reminded him.

He looked into his wife's face. A moment of joy sparked, but was quickly extinguished with the reminder of loss.

Lucina patted his back. "We shall feast in your honor tonight."

"Sounds wonderful. But first," he lifted his arm and smelled it, "I believe I need a bath."

Lucina chuckled. "Lea can help you wash and I'll see if I can find a change of clothes for you."

"You do have a cloak," Lea remembered. She

retrieved a wrapped package from her room and handed it to Timothy.

Unfolding it, he produced Paul's cloak and parchments. "I had nearly forgotten."

"Priscilla was able to secure them after…" She swallowed away the constriction in her throat. "I've kept them here ever since."

He held the treasures against his body. "Thank you."

The three feasted long into the night as if they had never eaten before.

After the first true night of decent sleep either man or woman had in two years, they said goodbyes to their sweet hostess and boarded a ship back to their beloved Ephesus.

When Lea's feet stepped on the familiar docks of home, she wanted to kiss the ground. Years in Rome and months aboard the last ships she ever hoped to sail on only fanned the flames of her love for the city she had known since childhood.

Timothy pulled Lea in close. "Home?"

"Home," she agreed.

They strolled the streets taking in every sight. The smells and sounds of the market called to them as they passed. Lea couldn't wipe the broad smile from her face.

When they made it to the door of the rented house, they paused.

"Should we knock or just go in?" Timothy

asked.

"It hasn't been our home in such a long time. Perhaps it's best to knock."

He lifted a hand and rapped on the wood.

The door cracked open and a familiar face filled the opening.

"Timothy?" Tychicus squinted at them. "Lea?"

"It is us."

He pressed himself forward and fell on their necks weeping. "Praise Yahweh!" he shouted and kissed them again. "We've been praying for you for so long."

"Your prayers have been heard."

"Come in and share with me all that has happened."

The couple recounted all their adventures from the moment they left till the moment their ship docked in port.

Tychicus sat soaking it all in and reliving every heart-piercing moment with them. "I suppose it's time to turn over the churches back to their rightful shepherd."

"Thank you for your service."

"Happy to be of help." He beamed. "I only wish my services weren't required for so long."

"How is Trophimus?" Lea asked.

"Finally recovered from his illness, I'm happy to report. He visits often."

"I've prayed for him and all of you."

Tychicus turned to Timothy. "There is something I need to share with you."

"Oh?"

"After word spread about Paul's death. Something happened here."

"The church?"

"The church actually grew. That's what I wanted to tell you. Due to the size of the harvest here in Ephesus, someone has come to help."

Timothy and Lea exchanged a glance.

"Who?"

"John."

"The disciple of Jesus?"

"The same. He brought Ima Mary with him as well."

"Jesus' mother?" Lea gasped. "She's here?"

"They've been living in Ephesus for the past year."

"Can we meet them?"

"Of course. I'll take you to them."

True to his word, Tychicus took them to John's home and made the introductions.

"I must let the elders know of your return," Tychicus said. "I'll leave you to get to know each other." He took his leave.

"Would you help me in the kitchen?" Ima Mary asked Lea.

"I'd be glad to."

Lea watched Ima Mary's skilled hands work. Though wrinkled by time, they never shook. She remembered watching Lois and Eunice with as much awe at the way the tasks seemed to come as easily as breathing. A life of service seemed to come more naturally with age.

"So, tell me," Ima Mary started. "What brings you to Ephesus?"

"I was actually born here." Lea rolled out some dough. "Spent most of my life within this city's limits."

"I thought Tychicus mentioned you had just come from Rome."

"We did." She paused. "We traveled there a few years ago to see my husband's mentor, Paul."

"Of Tarsus?"

"The same." She went back to kneading the dough. "He had been imprisoned and called for Timothy. So, we went."

"I was very sorry to hear of Paul's death. He was a good man."

"He was." A tear slipped down her cheek and she brushed it away. "I miss him very much."

Ima Mary patted her hand.

"My husband was then imprisoned as well. It was two years later that they finally released him. We came straight home."

"It sounds as though you've been through a great deal."

"We have." She wiped her face again. "But it's good to be home."

A knock at the door roused John to answer it.

"Mary?" he asked.

Lea looked at Ima Mary standing next to her.

Ima Mary perked up from her task and moved to the doorway between the kitchen and main area.

"Who is it?" Lea asked.

She stretched her neck to see around John. "Mary of Bethany. She is a follower of my son."

"It was awful." Mary of Bethany wept in the open doorway. Her ashen face was soaked with tears and her dress was covered in dust.

Lea came to stand next to Ima Mary. "It looks like she ran all the way here from Bethany."

"It wouldn't surprise me."

"Come in and sit down." John waved her inside.

"It's terrible. Just terrible."

Ima Mary poured a cup of cool water and handed it to John.

"You're safe now," John said, passing Mary of Bethany the cup.

"Just awful." Her hands shook around the cup. She spilled some on her chin as she took a sip and then put it down. "There was so much screaming and fire. John, the fire burned so large."

"From the beginning, tell me what happened."

"When General Vespasian became Emperor, he sent his son Titus to deal with the rebellion in Jerusalem. No one could get in or out of the city. I stayed in Bethany and prayed."

John nodded in understanding. "I spent much time in prayer as well."

"Then the machines came."

"Machines?"

"These giant structures that threw boulders at the walls. I could hear them all day." She shuttered. "It didn't take long before they made it through the walls. Smoke rose high from the city. The large, dark clouds hung over it. I saw a large smoke pillar coming from where the Temple stood. With the Romans' rage, it wouldn't surprise me at all if not one stone was—"

"—was left on another," John picked up her words.

She tilted her head.

He met her eyes. "You don't remember?"

Mary of Bethany searched her memory, but came up empty.

"Jesus told us. 'Not one stone will be left on top of another. Every one of them will fall.' We asked him later what He meant. He explained some of the signs of his coming."

"Yes! I remember now."

"He told us so much that we didn't understand," John said. "He even told us we wouldn't understand until later."

Mary of Bethany took a few deep breaths.

"When I saw the smoke coming from the city, I packed what I could carry and just started running." Her heart finally slowed. "I kept walking from town to town until I got to Ephesus. I remembered you had settled here and came to find you. I'm so tired."

"Rest," John said. "I will make sure you're safe. I'm sure the last thing the Romans are looking for is a Jewish woman."

John moved to the kitchen. "Poor thing has been through a nightmare. Would you mind fixing us something to eat? I need to speak with her."

Ima Mary set out a platter and started filling it.

Timothy entered. "Perhaps we should take our leave."

"So soon?" Ima Mary wondered.

"It seems you are both needed to tend to your guest. We have many more people to see."

"Of course. I want to take Mary of Bethany's testimony anyway." John went back into the main area.

"It was lovely to meet you." Lea kissed Ima Mary's cheek and squeezed her hand. "I'd like to visit again."

"Our door is always open to you."

Lea followed Timothy into the main area. She moved to Mary of Bethany and hugged her. "I pray you find peace here in Ephesus."

"Thank you."

Timothy walked Lea out and they headed

toward home.

"What do we do now?" she asked.

"What Paul asked of me in his last letter." He turned toward the street. "I'm going to start a training ministry right here in Ephesus."

Lea's heart lifted. She knew if others could be trained, the message would spread further than ever before. She knew with Paul gone Timothy was the one to carry the torch.

Epilogue

"For I am now ready to be offered, and the time of my departure is at hand. I have fought a good fight, I have finished my course, I have kept the faith:" -2 Timothy 4:6-7

81 A.D., Ephesus

Lea held onto Timothy's arm as they left the training meeting for the latest group of men. Her husband beamed with pride at their quick study and hunger to spread the message of the Way.

He patted her hand. "They will be ready sooner than the last group."

"Seems every group gets younger."

"It's just that we are getting older."

She swatted his shoulder. "Take that back."

"At least I'm getting older," he clarified. "You are more beautiful than the day I met you."

She blushed. "Neither of us is old. You simply have enough years behind you that no man questions your authority anymore."

"It took long enough."

Lea chuckled.

Music came from up Processional Way.

"What is all that noise?"

"Katagogia," the word tumbled from Timothy's lips. "I had completely forgotten the day. They are going to the theater."

A crowd of masked people headed toward them. The large ones, Lea assumed were males, waved clubs with broad ends in the air. Others held statues of gods.

Screams followed as the masked worshippers struck anyone passing by.

"I've put up with their rituals of carnage long enough." Timothy set his shoulders. "This ends today."

As the group moved toward them, a man lifted his club toward Lea.

Timothy moved between them, pushed Lea away, and restrained the man.

Others circled him and beat him with their clubs.

Lea heard the crunch of bone and screams for restraint. She shrieked and scrambled away.

Finding shelter behind a nearby building, she waited for the processional to pass.

When the streets emptied of the masked ones, she came out to find her husband's body lying lifeless. She laid on his chest and begged him to take a breath.

He did not.

As her tears dried, she set out for the only person she could think of.

"John," she whispered his name as he opened the door to her. "It's Timothy…"

"Take me to him."

John followed her to the place where Timothy's body lay to see for himself. He held her as they both wept. "I'll have his body buried."

A few days later, Lea sat in black sackcloth with John in her home. They both held their silence after seeing many of the Way followers leave for the day. They had come to remember Timothy and offer what help they could to the new widow.

John cleared his throat. "I've received news."

Lea snapped out of her daze and looked at him.

"I've been called to Rome."

The single word sent panic through her entire body. She bolted up. "You can't go there."

"I must." He waved his hand for her to sit. "I've been requested to appear before Emperor Domitian. With Ima Mary gone on to be with her son, there is no one here for me to worry about."

"What about me?"

John looked down at the table. "I meant no one who can't care for themselves." He looked up at her. "Besides, I've already sent word to Tychicus. He has agreed to come back to Ephesus to take over the church while I'm gone."

"Tychicus?"

"Seems he has taken a wife by the name of Jobina. He is looking forward to introducing the two of you."

Tears streamed down her face. "I can't let you go."

"With all due respect, Lea, it's not your place to keep me here."

Months passed as Lea adjusted into her new role serving alongside Tychicus and Jobina. The two women had accepted each other with grace and love from their first meeting. It was a smooth transition for Tychicus to keep up the work Timothy had been doing among the system of churches.

Jobina handed Lea a refreshing cup of cool water as they had finished tiding the house. Tychicus was due to return home soon and they wanted to have a meal ready for him the moment he entered.

The door opened and Tychicus appeared.

By his ashen face, Lea knew something was wrong.

"Who is it?" she begged.

He looked up at her and then back down.

"Who is it!"

He met her fiery gaze. "It seems John won't be returning as we hoped."

Tears blurred her vision. "What has happened?"

"On my way home, I was approached by a messenger from a member of the church in Rome. When John made it to Rome, Domitian ordered him to be killed by casting him into a cauldron of boiling oil."

Lea gasped and put both hands over her chest.

"He survived," Tychicus rushed on. "By some miracle, without injury."

"That's good."

"Not quite."

She held her head.

"It seems Domitian wasn't pleased with the result and has banished John to the Island of Patmos."

"Until?"

"Until his death."

Lea felt faint.

Jobina moved to her side and squeezed her arms. "Come sit down."

She obeyed.

"What does this mean?" Jobina asked her husband.

"It means there are no more carriers of the message."

"Yes, there are." Lea stood. "Everyone who poured into us is now with our Lord. It is up to us who remain to pour out what has been poured into us. All those whom Timothy trained and all those who heard the message from Paul. We all need to remain drink offerings for Jesus."

Tychicus and Jobina nodded.

"Paul and the other disciples, Priscilla and Aquila, my dear Timothy, and our beloved John. No matter how many shed their blood, the gospel will spread. They can burn our temple and kill our brothers and sisters, but they won't be able to stop the message of the Way. The other's stories will last as long as we speak about them, but the gospel will have a lasting legacy."

Loved the Faith Finders Series? Then you'll enjoy The Rebekah Series.

A stranger plagues Rebekah's dreams. Another offers her an unknown future.

Shepherding fills Rebekah's days with hard work and absorbed attention. Returning home to winter her flock brings back the nightmares that have haunted her since childhood.

After her father's tragic injury, he charges her with the task of training her younger brother to replace him. Will Laban learn from her or will her family's security be held in shaky hands?

When a stranger offers her another path, will she take it? Can she walk away from the family that depends on her for one she barely knows?

Follow Rebekah as she listens to the stranger's call in Book 1 of The Rebekah Series, *The Stranger*.

Also By Jenifer Jennings:

Special Collections and Boxed Sets
Biblical Historical stories from the Old Testament to the New, these special boxed editions offer a great way to catch up or to fall in love with Jenifer Jennings' books for the first time.

Faith Finder Series: Books 1-3
Faith Finders Series: Books 4-6
The Rebekah Series: Books 1-3
Servant Siblings Series: Books 1-3

* * *

Faith Finders Series:
Go deeper into the stories of these familiar faith heroines.

Midwives of Moses
Wilderness Wanderer
Crimson Cord
A Stolen Wife
At His Feet
Lasting Legacy

* * *

The Rebekah Series:
Follow Rebekah on her faith journey through life.

The Stranger
The Journey
The Hope

* * *

Servant Siblings Series:
*They were Jesus' siblings,
but they become His followers.*

James
Joseph
Assia
Jude
Lydia
Simon
Salome

* * *

Paul's Patrons Series:
Little known supporters of Paul's ministry have their own stories to tell.

Raging Sea
Warring Church

**Find these titles at your favorite retailer or at:
jeniferjennings.com/books**

Thank You!

Allison and Patrick, you were more than the inspiration for this book. I pray the heartbeats displayed on these pages beat with yours and the others out there who give their lives in service for the gospel.

Hubby, as always none of this would be possible without you. You've been my sounding board in the late hours of the night, my broad shoulder to weep on, my pick-me-up when life gets rough, my most valuable encourager, and the second love of my life only behind my Jesus. "I love you" isn't strong enough for what you mean to me, but it'll have to do.

Word Weavers Clay County, your prayers, critiques, excitement, and love have pushed me beyond myself. Thank you for sharing this writing journey with me.

Jenifer's Jewels (ARC Team), your love for my stories keeps me going. Knowing you're out there watching your emails for news of another story keeps me going when the writing gets rough. Thank you for loving the characters I create.

My dear readers, the biggest thank you of all goes

to you. This series was continued for those of you who have devoured each previous book. I'm so glad these stories came to life for you. Through every encouraging word, you pressed me to write more stories. I hope the other series I write stand next to the blaze of this one.

About the Author

Jenifer Jennings writes Historical novels that immerse readers in ancient worlds filled with Biblical characters and faith-building stories. Coming to faith in Jesus at seventeen, she spends her days falling in love with her Savior through the study of His Word. Jenifer has a Bachelor's in Women's Ministry and graduated with distinction while earning her Master's in Biblical Languages. When she's not working on her latest book, Jenifer can be found on a date with her hardworking husband or mothering their two children.

If you'd like to keep up with new releases, receive spiritual encouragement, and get your hands on a FREE book, then join Jenifer's Newsletter at:
jeniferjennings.com/gift

www.ingramcontent.com/pod-product-compliance
Lightning Source LLC
LaVergne TN
LVHW012147030225
802900LV00035B/802